"Did you know I was here?" he demanded. **"Or did you just get lucky?"**

"I wouldn't call this lucky."

Keira pulled emphatically on the rope around her arms, and in spite of himself, Graham winced.

"If you're not going to answer my questions," he said, "then I'm going to go back to our previous arrangement."

"What previous arrangement was that?" she replied, just shy of sarcastic.

"The one where I don't speak at all."

He started to turn away, but she snorted, and he stopped, midturn, to face her again.

"More of the silent treatment? What are you?" she asked. "A ten-year-old boy?"

For some reason, the question annoyed him far more than her lack of candor. Graham strode toward her, and once again, she didn't cower. She raised her eyes and opened her mouth, but whatever snarky comment had been about to roll off her tongue was cut off as Graham mashed his lips into hers messily. Uncontrollably. And when it ended, Keira was left gasping for air—gasping for *more*.

Trusting
a Stranger

MELINDA
DI LORENZO

MILLS
BOON®

First Published in Great Britain 2016
By Mills & Boon, an imprint of HarperCollins*Publishers*
1 London Bridge Street, London, SE1 9GF

Large Print edition 2016

© 2016 Melinda A. Di Lorenzo

ISBN: 978-0-263-06650-0

Printed and bound in Great Britain
by CPI Antony Rowe, Chippenham, Wiltshire

Melinda Di Lorenzo is a Canadian author living on the West Coast of British Columbia. She is an avid reader and an avid writer. Her to-be-read and to-be-written lists are of equal overwhelming length and she plans on living to be 150 years old so she can complete them both. Melinda is happily married to the man of her dreams and is a full-time mom to three beautiful girls. When she is not detangling hair, fighting for her turn on iTunes or catching up on sleep, she can be found at the soccer pitch or on the running trail.

As always, I owe the deepest gratitude
to my family. Without them,
I would never have been able to
add the title of "writer" to my list.

Prologue

Mike Ferguson crossed and uncrossed his legs, then crossed them again.

Even though the swanky hotel room was loaded with testosterone-fueled tension, the movement was the only indication that any of it affected him.

So far anyway.

Unflappable. It was a characteristic he valued above most others. A characteristic each of the two men in front of him lacked utterly.

The one with his meaty fingers around the other's neck…he was on edge. On *the* edge, maybe. He should've been calm. Self-assured. Those were the things that would make a man good at a job like his. Instead, he used ego and coercion tactics to get his way.

The one on his knees was just as bad. A blubbering mess. Or he would've been blubbering, if he'd been able to do more than gurgle. Had he shown a little more fortitude, the first man would've released him long ago and traded violence for a reasonable conversation.

Ferguson sighed.

Either way, both men were weak, as far as he was concerned. An embarrassment to work with.

Ferguson cared so little about them that he couldn't even be bothered with their names. Unfortunately, they were a necessity for this particular issue. Because they were also the only two men on the planet who knew as much as Mike did about his activities. The only two men who could implicate him for the one time in twenty years that he'd lost his cool while trying to protect everything he'd worked so hard to achieve.

"You think you found Mike Ferguson," the first man growled at the second. "What were you going to do about it? Turn me in?"

Gurgle, gurgle.

"Or were you going to tell our mutual friend and let *him* turn Mike in? Or maybe just skip the preamble and kill me?"

Gurgle, gurgle, gurgle.

"Fat chance you'd get to that badly disguised weapon of yours before my palm crushed your trachea."

Gurgle.

Ferguson was tired of the theatrics.

"Drop him." The command came out as if he was talking to a dog about a bone and, truthfully, it was kind of the way he saw them.

Beta dog. And even *more* beta dog.

The presently dominant one flexed his hand once more, then released the submissive one to the ground.

"You know I'd never turn him in," the second man croaked.

"We *all* know that," the first replied. "Takes a hell of a lot more guts than you've got to do the job that I do. You've been looking for Mike Ferguson for how long? And nothing. You couldn't find him until *I* let you."

"You think that's what happened?" The other man finally sounded a little gutsier. "I've suspected all along that he was under my nose. What I was looking for was *proof.* Because that's how *I* do things."

Ferguson rolled his eyes, came to his feet and stepped between them. "Your pissing contest is starting to get to me, boys."

"Waiting is starting to get to *me*," the first man snapped. "I want the other half of my money."

"Relax," said Ferguson. "Both of us want to be paid. And I agree. Enough time has passed, and we've all exercised enough patience for one lifetime. Your *friend* has stewed long enough. He needs to be smoked out."

"He'll never leave," said the second man. "And he's stupidly stubborn. Bad enough that if we go to him, he'll probably die before he tells you where he's hidden what you're looking for."

"So motivate him."

"Motivate him? It's been four years," pointed

out the first man. "I'm tired of hanging around, waiting for him to show his face, hoping he'll turn up and lead me to the painting. I think *I* could motivate him just fine."

Ferguson gritted his teeth. "This doesn't need muscle. It needs finesse."

He reached into his pocket and pulled out his preferred weapon of choice. Photographic evidence. He held it out, knowing it was far more menacing than any gun.

"You recognize the kid?"

"Yes!"

"His life is in your hands."

The man on the ground was immediately blubbering all over again. "Please don't!"

"Motivation," Ferguson stated coldly. "Just enough to get the man to his own house. Then we can decide whether we move on to muscle. Two days, no more. Understood?"

"Yes."

The reply was barely more than a whisper. It didn't have to be. Ferguson knew the beta dog had been motivated enough.

Chapter One

Keira Niles stepped on the gas, checked her rear-view mirror and smiled.

Admittedly, it was kind of a forced smile.

But it was a smile nonetheless.

Because today was going to be the day.

The one where she said yes.

The one where she gave in to Drew Bryant, the handsome, friendly neighborhood businessman whom she'd been flirting with for four years.

Today, she would tell herself—and believe it— that his business-minded attitude was a complement to her socially conscious one instead of a sharp contrast to it.

Yes, she was finally ready to dismiss the

doubts in her mind that had never seemed all that reasonable to start out with.

Drew was as close to a perfect man as she'd ever met. Calm and predictable, financially stable and kind. Tall enough that when they kissed for the first time, she'd probably have to tip her head up at least a little, and good-looking enough that he'd probably stay that way until both of them were too old to care anyway.

It was a good list. A good cross section of pleasant characteristics that were totally at odds with the nervous butterflies in her stomach.

Go away, Keira grumbled at them.

But no. She was nervous, and the butterflies were prevailing. So she did the only thing she could—she beat them down as forcibly as she knew how.

No more excuses, no more waiting for this, that or the other thing.

She straightened her dress over her thighs and glanced at her bare ring finger on the steering wheel one more time. Maybe soon it wouldn't look so naked and exposed. So free.

Don't be silly, Keira, she chastised herself.

But it wasn't that silly, if she thought about it.

Her parents would be happy if she settled down. They weren't getting younger, and neither was she. Or Drew. He was nearly forty, and he'd hinted enough times that he was just waiting for the right girl. He'd also hinted enough times that maybe *Keira* was that girl. Jokingly called her his girlfriend on repeat since he moved in beside her parents just a few years earlier.

He was a good, stable man. Handsome. Friendly. A catch.

Just this morning, when she'd come by to water her mom's rhododendrons, he'd paused to say goodbye before he left for his business trip. He'd given her a peck on the cheek—and while it hadn't lit her up with fireworks, it hadn't felt bad, either. It wasn't until he drove away that Keira saw that he'd left his briefcase behind.

And a man on a business trip needs his briefcase.

It was a sign. A subtle push that she ought to take a spontaneous, romantic leap.

After only the briefest hesitation, she'd decided to do it. No call, no warning. Just a seizing of the moment. So she grabbed the overnight bag she kept at her parents' house and set out on the four-hour trip to the Rocky Mountains and the aptly named Rocky Mountain Chalet.

It was a chilly oasis right in the middle of the mountains—a hot spot for honeymooners who preferred ski hills to sandy beaches and hot toddies to margaritas. The surrounding resort town had year-round residences, too, but the chalet was really the hub of activity.

It would've surprised Keira if her parents' soft-spoken neighbor had chosen a place like this for a weekend of business, but she doubted he'd picked it himself. His clients, who often stopped by his house, and whom she'd had only a few occasions to meet over the past few years, seemed like the kind of men who liked nice things. Bespoke suits and menus that didn't have any prices.

Not that Drew was any less classy. He was just a little more understated than overpriced. A little more golf shirt and chinos, and little less glossy necktie and cufflinks. A square-cut diamond versus a marquise.

You're stalling.

Keira realized that she *had* stopped, her hands on the wheel at exactly ten and two, her eyes so glazed over that they almost didn't see the forbidding sign that pointed out cheerily how solidly she was about to seal her fate.

No Turnaround, Twenty-Two Miles, it read.

The drive time had passed far more quickly than she thought. The hours had felt like minutes, and the resort was close now.

Was what she was doing crazy and impetuous? Maybe. But it was also the perfect story to tell their friends. Their kids, if they had them. Plus, she got the feeling that settling into a life with Drew wouldn't allow a whole lot of wildness.

Which is a good thing, she reminded herself.

She was mild mannered and easygoing, too. So they were kind of perfect for each other.

And she was almost there. That final turn up the mountain was all it would take.

"Well," she said to the air. "This is it."

Somehow, the second she clicked on her turn signal, the air got colder.

And when she depressed the gas pedal and actually followed through on the turn itself, Keira swore she had to turn the heat up.

GRAHAM WOKE FROM the nightmare far too slowly.

It was the kind of dream that he deserved to be ripped away from quickly, not dragged from reluctantly.

In it, he'd been chasing Holly through their home. She'd started out laughing, but her laughter had quickly turned to screams, and when Graham caught up with her at the bottom of the curved staircase, he saw why. Sam's small body was at the bottom. Graham had opened his mouth to ask what Holly had done, but she beat him to it.

"What did you *do?"*

The words were full of knowing accusation,

and try as he might, he couldn't deny responsibility for the boy's death.

The image—and the question—hung in Graham's mind as he eased into consciousness.

In reality, he'd never seen Sam's body—just the aftermath and the blood.

In the dream, though, it was always the same. Holly alive and Sam dead, and Graham left broken and unable to shake the false memories. He wished desperately that they would disappear completely, or at least fade as he opened his eyes. Instead, they tightened and sharpened like a noose around his psyche.

Survivor's guilt.

Graham was sure that was a large part of what he felt. The problem was he was increasingly sure he *wasn't* surviving.

The leads had dried up long ago, his investigation into who had pulled the trigger growing frustratingly colder with each year.

Even the name—Michael Ferguson—the one thing he'd had to go on, had never panned out.

Graham had always believed the truth would

come out and, with it, justice. It had never been a part of his plan to live out his days—to *survive* them—in the middle of the woods in a cabin no one knew existed. He sure as hell never thought he'd wake some mornings wondering if he was as guilty as everyone thought he was.

What kind of man admitted publicly that he didn't love his wife just days after being accused of her murder?

Did an innocent man escape police custody and promptly disappear?

In the early days, those questions seemed easy to answer.

An innocent man ran only so he could give the authorities enough time to *prove* his innocence.

Four years had gone by, though, and instead of gaining traction and credibility, Graham's story had at first exploded in hatred and bitterness. Then faded to obscure infamy.

Dreams like the one he'd just had made him question every choice he'd made since the second he picked up his cell phone on that morning.

What if he hadn't answered it at all?

What if he'd called 9-1-1 himself instead of giving that nosy neighbor the time to do it?

What if—

The squawk of Graham's one and only electronic device cut off his dark thoughts. The bleep of the two-way radio was so unexpected that he almost didn't recognize it.

The mountain range that held the cabin hostage also insulated the location from uninvited transmissions. The two-way mounted to the underside of Graham's bed could only be reached one of two ways. Either the message sender had to be less than a hundred feet away, or he had to be right beside the tower at the top of the mountain, tuned to exactly the correct frequency.

The first would mean initiating lockdown mode. Which Graham wasn't in the mood for.

The second meant someone was trying to reach him on purpose.

And only one person knew where he was.

"G.C., do you read me?"

Dave Stark. A friend. A confidant. The only person who'd stuck by him over the years. He was the man who'd placed the call to Graham on *that* morning. Whose voice threw Graham back every time he heard it.

"You there?" Dave asked.

Graham swung his legs from the bed and reached down to flip the switch.

"I should be asking if *you're* there. And why you're calling me sixteen days ahead of schedule. We're regimented for a reason."

"G.C., stop being your bullheaded self for one second… I have good news."

Graham went still. *Good* news? He wasn't sure what to do with the statement.

"Come again?"

"I found the man we've been looking for."

The world spun under Graham's feet. His mouth worked silently. Four years of waiting to hear those words, and now that he had, he couldn't think of a single damned thing to say.

"You still there, G.C.?"

Graham cleared his throat. "Where is he?"

"A place you know well."

"Stop being cagey, Dave. It doesn't suit you. Or the situation."

"Home."

Home. Forty-nine miles of nearly inaccessible terrain and two hundred more of straight highway driving is all that stands between you and the man who very likely killed your wife and son, and robbed you of your life. Michael damned Ferguson.

Hmm. Graham was far from stupid. What were the odds? And why had he surfaced now?

"He's there on business. Must've thought enough time had gone by that no one would be looking," Dave added as if in answer to Graham's silent question. "Booked in a hotel under another name, but I swear to God, G.C., I'd recognize the man in my sleep."

"You've got the snowmobile ready to go?" Graham asked.

There was the slightest pause. "Yeah. But there's a weather advisory out. They're expecting a blizzard and the whole town is shut down already. No one can get in or out. Blockades up and everything."

"You can't get around them?"

Another pause. "Of course I can. But I won't. Had to flash my ID just to get away long enough to come up to the tower."

"So flash it again."

"It's taken me this long to find him, I don't want to get caught because of a stupid decision. The blockades will be up all night, and probably into tomorrow. If it's clear enough by morning, I'll find a way out. One that won't arouse the suspicion of every rent-a-cop in the area."

"If he gets away—"

"He won't. His hotel reservation in Derby Reach is good until Wednesday morning, G.C., and I paid the clerk a hundred bucks to watch him. Two full days is plenty of time."

Graham stifled his frustration. "Fine."

"Over and out."

By the time the radio screeched, then went silent, Graham was already pulling clothes from his freestanding closet. No way was he waiting another twenty-four hours to get to Dave.

And Ferguson.

Chapter Two

Keira stepped on the gas and squinted into the snowy onslaught, then glanced in the rearview mirror, trying desperately to see...anything. It was a hopeless endeavor. Someone could be right on her bumper, and she wouldn't know the difference.

Just minutes after she pulled her car onto the road that led up to the resort, the big, friendly flakes had turned into tiny, angry ones that threatened her vision.

Then she'd heard the announcement. They were closing the roads down. Emergency access only. She couldn't turn around, even if she wanted to. She just prayed that she'd get there in one piece.

In fact, if her calculations were right, she was kind of sure she should *already* have gotten there.

She gripped the wheel tightly.

The terrain underneath her car seemed to be growing steadily more uneven and the front-wheel drive hybrid was starting to protest.

But she pushed on.

"So much for signs," she muttered, and shot Drew's briefcase a dirty look.

Keira looked at the rearview again.

If someone was behind her, would they be able to see her, even with the lights on?

Unconsciously, she pushed down on the gas again, and her car heaved underneath her.

"C'mon, you stupid thing," she muttered. "Any second we'll reach the turnoff for the resort and you can go back to being your eco-obsessed self again."

After another few minutes of driving, the trees on the other side of the road still hadn't thinned out, and there was no break in the blizzard.

It really did seem to be a blizzard now. Even

though it was technically daylight, the whiteness of the snow somehow darkened everything in Keira's line of vision.

So that's what a whiteout *means.*

She flicked on her high beams. They made no difference.

At last, Keira turned to the logical voice in her head for guidance.

Its reply was an unexpected shout.

Moose!

The huge, hairy beast stood out against the blank whiteness. It stared down the car. And it wasn't moving.

It's not moving!

"I know, dammit!" Keira yelled back at the voice.

She swung the steering wheel as hard as she could. In reply, the tires on the hybrid screeched their general disapproval of the maneuver. As the speedometer dropped down to ten miles an hour, the car skidded past the moose and, for just a moment, relief flooded through Keira's body. But when she tore her eyes away from the animal, she saw that she'd simply traded in one di-saster for another. A yawning chasm beckoned to her hybrid.

And all she could do as she sailed over the edge was close her eyes and pray.

As GRAHAM STOMPED through the ever-thickening storm, his feet grew heavier. Even his snow-shoes seemed to protest the slow trek. The route was steep and a lot of it bordered on treacher-ous. The bonus was that vertical climb turned a forty-mile hike into a ten-mile one instead.

Sweat built up on Graham's skin, dripping down his face and freezing in his beard. He flicked away the ice and paused to take a breath. The air was cold enough to burn. But neither the snow nor the wind were enough to block out the raging of his thoughts.

You knew the storm was coming but you picked this path anyway and you don't have a damned thing to complain about. You're sure as hell not giving up.

He slammed down his snowshoes with even more force and moved on. His internal monologue was right in so many more ways than he'd meant it to be. He hadn't just picked this particular path at this particular moment. He'd picked all the paths that led up to the metaphorical storm—perfectly matched to the actual one—which was his life.

The king of bad decisions.

With a crown of regret.

He almost laughed. Today of all days was not the day to turn into a poet.

Been alone far too long, he thought.

Then he *did* laugh. Solitude was so much more than a choice. It was an absolute necessity.

So, no. He didn't need poetry or cynicism or even hope. Cold, hard facts. That was where this was leading. A long-awaited resolution.

He laughed again, and the rumble of his baritone chuckle punctuated the cold air for just a second before the wind cut through and carried it away. As the laugh faded, another rumble followed it, this one far deeper, and so loud it echoed over the sound of the storm.

Graham froze.

An avalanche?

This thought was quickly overridden as he realized the noise was actually a human one.

A car engine and tires on the icy pavement.

It had been years since he'd been close enough to any kind of traffic to hear the sound. Graham's eyes lifted in search of the road above. With the snow as heavy as it was, he couldn't see anything more than a few feet ahead.

The rumble continued, growing even louder.

What kind of maniac is out in these conditions? Graham wondered, then shook his head.

Clearly someone who had even less regard for their own safety than he did.

Graham took another few steps, expecting the noise to fade away. It didn't. In fact, it seemed to be building. And then it stopped abruptly.

Something wasn't right.

Graham's ears strained against the muted broil

of the storm and caught a high-pitched shriek, almost indiscernible from the wind. Then his eyes widened. The horizon was blank no more.

A purple streak shot off the cliff above, crashed through the trees, dropping first a dozen angled feet, then another ten. Then—incredibly, unbelievably—it slammed to the forest floor somewhere ahead.

Move!

He didn't stop to think about the consequences, but tore across the snow, beating branches out of his way as he ran. He was too determined to reach the site of the crash to let his awkward, snowshoed gait slow him, and in only a few minutes, he reached the car.

A girl.

He went very still for a very long second.

The driver was a young woman. With a flaming crown of auburn hair and her head pressed into the steering wheel, arms limp at her side.

The smell of gasoline was all around him, and the threat of explosion was very real.

And Graham felt something shift inside him. Every part of him that had gone numb with shock now went wild with a need to save her.

Chapter Three

Keira couldn't open her eyes. She had no idea if minutes had passed or if had been hours. She only knew that she was cold. Frozen right through her secondhand, designer sweater and her teeny-tiny dress to the bare skin beneath. A little pseudodrunkenly, she wondered why she hadn't dressed for the weather.

She should probably move. Try to get warm. But the chill was the bone-freezing kind that makes it impossible to move anything but chattering teeth.

Sleep threatened to take her, and though she knew instinctively that she should fight it, she was really struggling to find a good reason to stay awake.

The click of a seat belt drew her attention.

A car.

Her car. She was driving. Then falling.

Now she was being lifted.

Good.

But her relief was short-lived.

Next came the ripping, and the tearing off, of her clothes.

I'm being attacked.

The assumption slammed home fear and brought with it a burst of furious energy. Keira's arms came up defensively while her feet lashed out with as much aggression as she could muster. She wasn't going down without a fight.

Her knee connected with something solid, and for a moment she was triumphant.

Her eyes flew open, and this time when she froze, it was from something other than cold.

A pair of dark-lashed eyes, so gray they were almost see-through, stared back at her. They were set in a fully bearded face, partially obscured by a knitted hat, and they were pained. And angry. Furious, even.

Keira tried to shy back from their icy rage, but she was positioned in a deep dip in the frozen ground, and the hard-packed snow all around her was as unyielding as the man above her.

Roll over! Roll away!

Except she couldn't. Because the man had one hand over her collarbone. His palm was just shy of the base of her throat.

"Please," she gasped around the pressure he was exerting just below her trachea. "Please don't hurt me."

His eyes widened in surprise. Then very, very slowly, he shook his head. Then he let go of her neck. Cold air whipped across the exposed skin, making her shiver uncontrollably.

The man pulled away and disappeared from view. And the *r-r-r-rip* of fabric started up again immediately.

Oh, God.

In spite of the way Keira's body was shaking, she attempted to sit up. But in less than the time it took to draw in one ice-tinged breath, the man's hand shot out once more, closing over the same spot he'd released just moments earlier. He pursed his lips, and in spite of the cover of the beard, Keira could see the frustrated set of his jaw. He shook his head again.

What did he mean? Did he want her to just lie there while he stripped her down?

Keira didn't realize she'd spoken aloud until he nodded.

She tried to tell him she wouldn't do it—that she *couldn't* do it—but when she opened her mouth, the wind swept in and cut the words away.

She thought he must've taken her silence as acquiescence, because he disappeared again, and suddenly Keira was stripped almost completely bare. Her dress had been so skimpy that she hadn't even bothered with a bra. And without the dress, all she had left were her lacy boy-cut undies, and if she remembered correctly, they didn't leave much to the imagination.

Very abruptly, Keira didn't feel cold anymore.

She had a bizarre urge to look down and check if her panties were as revealing as she believed them to be.

Not a good sign.

She tried to lift her arms, and when she found them to be too leaden to move, frustration shot through her.

"I need to see my panties!"

The words came out in an almost shout, and they struck Keira as hilarious. A giggle burst from her lips.

The bearded man was at her side in an instant, concern evident on his face. Keira thought *that* was funny, too. One second he had her by the throat, the next he was worried about her.

"What are you staring at, hmm, Mountain Man?" she asked.

Her laughter carried on, and even though it sounded a little hysterical, she still couldn't stop it.

The man stood up abruptly. From her position on the ground, Keira could see he was huge. Strikingly tall. Wide like a tree trunk.

And he was dressed in clothes that her mind couldn't make sense of. His enormous shoulders were draped in white fur, but underneath that was a Gore-Tex jacket. The hat—which she'd noted before—was incredibly lopsided and almost laughable. His pants were leather, but not the kind you'd find on a biker or on badly dressed club rat. Tucked into boots crafted of the same suede and held together with wide, sinewy stitches, they looked like something out of a seventh-grade social studies textbook.

Keira's giggles finally subsided, but only because her jaw had dropped to her chest.

In a move that made Keira concerned for his safety, the man began to undress.

What the heck?

He tossed the weird ensemble off without finesse.

For several long, inappropriate seconds, Keira had an opportunity to admire his naked form. Her gaze traveled the breadth of his muscled torso, taking in the cut of perfectly formed muscle. He had well-defined pecs and biceps, and a puckered scar just above his left collarbone.

Unclothed, he looked less like a mountain man and more like…well, more like a mountain itself.

Keira's eyes moved south, even though she knew she should stop them. Just as her gaze reached his belly button, though, he tossed the long underwear–style T-shirt he'd had under his jacket in her direction. It ballooned up, then settled about four inches above her head, suspended there by the walls of the dip where she was lying.

Before Keira could ask what he was doing, the man dove in beside her.

Very quickly, he slipped his boots onto her feet, then used the rest of his clothes to build a cocoon around them. His pants hung over their chests. The white fur that had been on his shoulders covered their legs and feet.

When he was done, he rolled Keira over forcefully. He wrapped the jacket around them and pulled her back into his chest. The world seemed to be vibrating, and it took her a long moment to realize it was because she was still shivering.

Without her permission, Keira's body wriggled into the stranger's, trying to absorb all the heat he was emitting. She attempted to fight it. She told her hips they shouldn't fit against his legs so perfectly. She mentally commanded her head not to tuck into the crook of his arm.

But it was a losing battle.

He inhaled deeply. And with his exhale, he flung his free arm over her waist and dragged her even closer. His bare leg slipped between Keira's newly booted feet and she couldn't even pretend to fight the need to be right there, exactly like that.

At long last, her shaking subsided.

Don't fall asleep.

But that, too, was an inevitability.

Great. Crash your car, then get stripped down and forcibly cuddled by an equally crazy man. Only you, Keira.

His heat lulled her. His solidity comforted her. His presence made her feel unreasonably safe.

And as she drifted off, she finally clued in to the Mountain Man's intentions. He wasn't trying to hurt her at all. He was just trying to keep her warm.

And he was very likely saving her life.

NAKED FLESH PRESSED to naked flesh. The oldest trick in the Boy Scout handbook for staving off hypothermia. It was effective, too, judging from the amount of heat in the snowy alcove.

The girl beside Graham adjusted a little, and one of her hands grazed his thigh.

Okay maybe Boy Scout *is the wrong choice of words*, Graham amended.

Every bit of movement reminded Graham that he was the furthest thing from a do-gooder kid in a uniform. Especially now that the panic that she was going to die on his hands had worn off.

The girl shifted beside him once again, wriggling ever closer and heightening his awareness of her petite form all the more. Her mess of auburn hair tickled his chest, and its light scent wafted to his nose. Her silky skin caressed him.

I'm in hell, Graham decided. *The worst kind of hell.*

She murmured something soft and breathy in her sleep, and Graham groaned.

Saving her might have been a mistake. An impetuous decision fueled by the man he used to be.

That...and her pretty face.

Her still, lifeless body behind the wheel had been almost too much for him to bear.

Bend. Lift. Drag.

She was easy to carry. So small. Almost fragile looking. Fair in that way that redheads often are, but with no smattering of freckles. In fact, the paleness of her skin rivaled the snow, and Graham wasn't sure whether it was a natural pallor, or something brought on by the accident and the cold. It didn't matter; she was entrancing.

Then he'd pulled her into the clearing, shaking and shivering and seemingly so needful.

Graham grimaced. She *was* beautiful, no doubt, but she definitely wasn't frail. An accident like that should have killed her. Coming out alive was a feat. But the fight in her when she'd woken up…that was a whole other story. It had impressed him as much as it had ticked him off.

Under the fine bones of her face, she was a firecracker, no doubt about it.

Graham slipped his hand to hers, touching the soft pad of her open palm, just because he could.

And because you want *to*, scolded an internal voice that sounded a little too much like his late grandmother.

It was true, though. He did want to. It had been a long time since his fingers last found residence in someone else's hand.

The girl's hand closed reflexively, and Graham jerked away.

Nice work, he thought. *Save a girl, then get creepy. You could at least wait until she tells you her name.*

Her name.

He felt an impatient compulsion to know what it was and, after just a second of considering it, he decided to see if he could find out. Maybe check for her ID in the car. She was warm enough now that she wasn't at risk of dying,

and he could safely give her—both of them—
some space.

He pushed aside his clothes-turned-blanket
and tucked them around the girl's body. Then
he slipped from the dip in the ground, stood silently and surveyed the area. The cold air buf-
feted against his skin, but he was accustomed
to the weather, and as he came to his feet, the
strong breeze in his eyes bothered him more
than the temperature did. The storm had slowed
quite a bit. The snow was light, mostly blowing
around from the residual wind.

He glanced down at the girl and adjusted the
overhanging shirt so she wasn't bared to the el-
ements. She'd be fine alone for a few minutes
while Graham had a closer look at her car and
attempted to figure out who she was. Then he'd
have to decide whether it was better to keep her
close, or try to get her back into town.

Into town.

In the heated excitement of saving her, meeting up with Dave had gone out of his head. In

fact, *everything* had gone out of his head, and he wasn't sure how that was possible.

Graham turned back to the girl.

In the past four years, his pursuit of justice had been relentless. Single-minded to the point of mania. He'd thought of nothing but finding the man who took Holly and Sam from his life. Now, very suddenly, he was distracted from his purpose.

By this girl.

He took another step closer to the car. The front end dipped down from the pressure exerted by Graham's body as he'd clambered across it on his insane rescue mission. The purple paint had been slashed to hell by the branches surrounding it, and the rear wheels were completely flat. Remarkably, the rest of the car was intact.

Graham stood underneath the vehicle, frowning. Damned lucky. The vehicle could have smashed to pieces, taking the girl with it. Or she could've gone off the road just a few miles up, and Graham would never have found her. She had to have some incredible karma stored up.

What if someone's waiting for her?

Graham's gut roiled. He had to assume that time wasn't a luxury he had. The second they— whether it was an emergency crew or someone else—found that car in its weirdly whole state, with its empty driver's seat, the relatively far distance to his place in the woods grew that much smaller.

Get control, man, he commanded himself.

He needed a plan.

His gaze sought the car and the spot where the girl lay hidden. A small, greasy puddle—presumably the source of the gasoline smell—had formed under the driver's side door and it gave him an idea.

They can't find the car in one piece.

He would make it harder for anyone to locate her. Harder to locate him.

Graham squinted up at the sky. Clouds obscured the waning sun.

Graham didn't own a watch. It had been years since the batteries in his old one wore out, and it had never seemed like much of necessity. Right that moment, though, he wished he had one so he could pinpoint the hour, predict the sunset and time it just right.

But you don't *have one*, he said to himself. *And you don't have time to wait, either.*

All he needed was a spark. One that could easily be generated with some of the electrical wires in the car engine.

Once he got started, it took less than an hour for Graham to render Keira's car satisfactorily unidentifiable. The dark, sour-smelling smoke was already dissipating, though he was sure he still reeked of fuel himself.

He took a step back to survey his handiwork once more. He thought it looked as natural as any burning car could. A branch puncturing the fuel line, the angle of the car conveniently leaking accelerant from the line to the engine, and the rest had gone up in smoke.

So to speak.

Graham was actually a little surprised at how efficiently the fire took hold. Not to mention how well the whole thing cooperated. Several minutes of blistering, blue-green flames, an enormous puff of black smoke, then a fade-to-gray cloud that blended in nicely with the fog that had rolled in from above.

Not that Graham was complaining—it sure as hell made his task a lot easier. The husk of the car continued to smolder, but with the fuel burned up and the decidedly frozen state of the surrounding area, he wasn't even worried about it spreading any farther.

Not bad for my first arson attempt.

The thought only made him smile for a second. The last thing he needed was to add another felony to the list that already followed his name around.

"Is that my car?"

At the soft, tired-sounding question, Graham whipped around. For a second, he just stared down at her, mesmerized by the way her long, dark eyelashes brushed against her porcelain skin, and entranced by the enticing plumpness of her lips.

He'd never seen a more beautiful girl, or felt an attraction so strong.

"Is it?" she said again.

Reality hit Graham.

Saving her had been a hell of a lot more than just a *bad* idea. If Graham's instincts were right—and they usually were—then this walk in the storm turned impromptu rescue mission… would be his undoing.

Chapter Four

Keira met the stranger's wary gaze with one of her own. For a moment she saw something heated and intriguing in his eyes that cut through the cold air and sizzled between them. Then it was gone, replaced by the guarded look he wore now, and Keira was left wondering if she'd imagined it.

Maybe it was a hallucination brought on by a head injury, she thought.

Her brain did feel fuzzy, and when she blinked, the snowy world swam in front of her. Even the big man—who was as solid a thing as she'd ever seen—seemed to wobble. Then a wicked, head-to-toe shiver racked Keira's body, and the

Mountain Man's face softened with worry. Very quickly, he undid his own big red jacket and stepped closer to offer it to her.

Keira only hesitated for a second before she took it gratefully. She vowed silently to give it back as soon as she was thawed. But right then, it was warm *and* it offered her a decent amount of cover, and with it wrapped around her body, she felt a little more in control. Still woozy. But better.

"My car..." Her voice sounded hoarse, and her throat burned a little as she spoke.

When the Mountain Man didn't answer her third inquiry, she tipped her head toward the smoking mess of metal, then looked back at him again. He just stared back at her, a little crease marking his forehead.

Keira let out a rasping sigh. "Do you speak English?"

He nodded curtly.

"So...what? You're just testing me out? Deciding if I'm *worthy* of speaking to?"

Her question earned a crooked smile. An expression that said, *Yeah, that's about right.*

Keira sighed again. A few silent hours with this stranger, and she could understand him perfectly. She doubted she could read Drew that easily, and she'd known him for years.

Drew.

Damn. A kicked-in-the-gut feeling made her shiver once more, and the Mountain Man reached out a hand, but she waved him off.

"I'm fine," she lied.

He raised an eyebrow. *Liar.*

"I don't care if you believe me or not," Keira stated. Her eyes narrowed with an irritation to cover her embarrassment, and then she muttered, "I'm just not used to sitting nearly naked in the snow."

He chuckled—a low, attractive sound that warmed her inexplicably—sat back on his heels and waited. Those piercing gray eyes of his demanded answers, and Keira found herself wanting to tell him the truth.

Her job as a child and youth counselor had

given her the ability to form good, quick judgments. And something in this man's handsome face made her think she could trust him.

Handsome?

The descriptor surprised Keira, and if her blood had been pumping through her body properly, she might've blushed.

Because yes, he *was* handsome.

He had full lips, an even brow and in spite of his facial hair, he had strong features. Keira was close enough to him that as she realized just how attractive he was, her heart fluttered nervously in her chest.

She was alone with him. In the middle of nowhere. She was injured. Maybe badly. And now she was remembering that glimpse she'd caught of his muscular torso when he'd stripped off his clothes so he could warm her up. Keira had been too out of it to think about it before. She was wishing she could see it again so she could memorize it.

What's the matter with you? she chastised herself.

She couldn't remember the last time she'd looked at a man like this. At least not long enough to notice how prettily translucent his eyes were, or how their wintry appeal so sharply contrasted with his burly frame. She certainly hadn't come close enough to one to know how well his body fit beside her, or how comfortable it was to be in his arms.

No way could Drew come close to this kind of magnetism.

Mountain magnetism.

And he was watching her again, that same not-so-muted heat in his eyes.

Maybe he's remembering the way you *felt cuddled up beside* him.

That thought was finally enough to draw the color to her cheeks, and Keira could feel the heat spread from her face down her throat and across her chest. She was sure she must be the same shade of red as the borrowed coat.

In an attempt to ease the increasingly palpable tension between them, Keira shifted her gaze back to her smoldering car.

Midway between the vehicle and spot where she was sitting a black flash caught her eyes.

My phone.

She knew that's what it was, and that she had to get it. And for some reason, she also knew that her benefactor—if his intentions were even good enough to call him that—wouldn't let her just go grab it. Not willingly.

Butterflies beat against Keira's stomach as she offered him a weak smile.

"Can you excuse me for a second?" Her voice was weak, even to her own ears. "I think I need to…uh…use the ladies' room."

GRAHAM NARROWED HIS EYES and considered calling her bluff. He was sure whatever reason she had for suddenly getting up, it had little to do with the most basic of physical needs.

Graham had to admit that he was surprised she could stand at all. What surprised him more, though, was that she took off into the dark. The borrowed boots flew off, and she moved at a hobbling, barefoot run.

What the hell?

Graham was so startled that he almost forgot he should chase her down. He stared after her, a puzzled frown on his face. Her creamy legs poke out from under the big coat, as sexy as they were ridiculous.

She really should tuck those away before she ruined them with frostbite, he thought absently.

She glanced over her shoulder at him and stumbled forward a little farther.

Where the hell did she think she was going? Her ridiculous flight was going to run her straight into the thickest part of the forest. It was going to tear up those pretty little feet of hers. And was going to create unnecessary work for Graham.

First World, fugitive-about-to-turn-kidnapper problems.

Still, Graham might've been tempted to let her go a little longer if he hadn't spied the wound on her thigh.

Dammit, he growled mentally.

How had he not noticed the slash before?

Her movement across the snow opened up the cut, and even from a few dozen feet away, Graham could see the blood ooze out of it.

Belatedly, he jumped to his feet and strode after her, his long legs closing the gap between them.

In seconds, he was on her, and without preamble he reached down, wrapped his arms around her knees and threw her unceremoniously over his shoulder. She beat weakly at his back, but he ignored it.

"Let me *go*!" Her order was almost a squeal, and Graham ignored that, too.

He carried her across the ground like a sack of potatoes, and when he had her right back at the spot she'd run from moments earlier, he dumped her to the ground—not quite hard enough to hurt, but just hard enough for her to squeak.

He shot her a look that commanded her to keep still and, although her eyes flashed, she didn't try to get up again. From the shallowness of her breathing and the deep flush in her cheeks, Graham doubted she *could* get up.

But as soon as he leaned back, she was off at a crawl.

If we were at the hospital, Graham thought, *I'd insist that an orderly strap her down.*

For a moment, he considered calling after her.

No. Speaking to her will only create more issues. Make you slip up and give something away. Too much risk.

He watched her shimmy helplessly over the snow for another second—she barely got more than a few inches—then stretched out, closed a hand over one of her ankles and dragged her back.

He righted her, set her between his thighs and held her there.

Using his teeth, Graham tore his T-shirt into strips—one to bind her hands together, another to bind her feet together, and a third to stop the flow of blood from her thigh. She fought him on the first two things—and he couldn't blame her for that—but when she finally spotted the wound, she stopped struggling.

Graham could feel her eyes following the

quick, sure movements of his hands as he fashioned the stretchy cotton into a tourniquet. He was disappointed that the blood soaked through almost immediately. He tore off another strip from his T-shirt, bundling the wrapping as thick as he could and as tight as he dared.

The flow of blood ebbed, but she was going to need stitches, and Graham had nothing on hand that would do the job.

"Mountain Man?" Her voice was soft. "I'm really hurt, aren't I?"

Graham nodded curtly.

She was silent for a minute, leaning her back into his chest. Then she shifted a little, tipping her head just enough that he could see her tempting, pink lips.

"I should warn you," she murmured. "I'm not going to make this easy."

Graham rolled his eyes. As if *that* surprised him.

In spite of her words, though, she turned sideways and settled her face against him. Then her eyelids fluttered shut, and her knees curled up as if she *belonged* in his lap.

With a frustrated groan, Graham tried to ease away, but the sleeping girl wriggled closer and then she murmured something else, and instead of trying to disentangle himself from her, Graham found himself straining to hear what it was. He tucked the coat over her legs and leaned down, pressing his face close to hers.

She shifted in his lap, and her lips brushed his ear.

Graham's body reacted immediately. Desire shot through him, and his grip on her tightened.

Slowly, he untied her wrists. He breathed out, waiting for her to wake up, realize she was free and level a punch at his face. Instead, she flexed one free hand, then slipped it up to his shoulder, her thumb grazing his collarbone.

Graham groaned and crushed down the ridiculous longing coursing through him.

A lock of auburn hair slipped to her cheek. Graham reached to brush it away reflexively. When his hand slid against her cheek, he realized the heat he felt could be blamed on more than just desire. Her skin was hot to the touch, and though her face was still pale, two spots of pink had bloomed in her cheeks.

Graham frowned and placed the back of his hand on her forehead, then trailed a finger down her face. Yeah, she was definitely far warmer than she ought to be.

He needed to get her somewhere safer, cleaner and functional enough for treatment. The clinic in the resort town was out of the question. Anywhere public was.

Home.

It was the best option.

Graham glanced up at the sky. The sun had completely set, and the sky was pitch-black. Travel now would be dangerous.

More dangerous, he corrected silently.

The climb down was steep, and he would have to carry her. Graham had no idea how long he'd be able to do that.

He looked back to the girl.

He didn't have any other choice.

Whatever circumstance had brought her to him, she was still in need of medical care, and however long ago it had been, Graham still held fast to his oath.

First do no harm.

Chapter Five

The ground beneath Keira was moving. It thumped along rhythmically like a conveyor belt made of nearly smooth terrain. It was soothing. Almost.

A sudden bump jarred her and sent her head reeling. Her eyes flew open, and the world was upside down. She realized it wasn't the ground that was moving. It was *her*. Them.

The big man had her cradled in his arms, and he was traveling across the snowy ground at an alarming speed. She could see the bottom of his bearded chin. His neck was exposed and a sheen of sweat covered it. His breathing was a little heavy, but he seemed oblivious to her added weight.

"Excuse me?" Keira's voice was far weaker than she wanted it to be, and if he heard her, he didn't acknowledge it.

She struggled to right herself, the quick pace making it difficult for her to do more than lift her head. All she could see was sky.

She blinked, and the sky stayed. The expanse of it was so big above her that it was almost dizzying. No moon. No stars. Just a solid spread of grayness. Keira closed her eyes to block it out as she tried to orient herself.

The big, red jacket was still wrapped around her, cinched at the waist and tied at the throat. A scarf was wound tightly around her head, insulating her face as well as her skull. The Mountain Man had used the white fur to cover both her feet and her legs. She wasn't in danger of freezing anymore, though the terrible cold she'd felt right before slipping into oblivion wasn't completely gone.

She felt weak. Really weak. She sought something tangible to grasp at in her sea of straw-like thoughts.

Wrists tied together. Not that. *Blood.* No. *The smoky, woodsy scent of the Mountain Man's skin.* Definitely not.

And at last she found something.

My phone. Yes.

She'd managed to grab it in her stumble across the snow. She'd shoved it into the coat pocket just seconds before the Mountain Man caught her and hoisted her over his shoulder, caveman-style.

Was it still there?

She desperately wanted to reach into the coat to find out.

But right that second, her hands—which were no longer bound together, she noted—were actually *under* his shirt, pressed into his nearly rock-hard chest. And there was no hope of drawing away with any chance of subtly. Her fingers fluttered nervously, and even though he didn't react, Keira was sure the stranger's pulse jumped with the movement.

Curiosity fueled her to see if she was correct.

She uncurled her fingers slowly and moved her

palm up, just an inch. The big man's heart was already working hard with exertion, but there was no mistaking the double beat as her hand came to rest on his sternum.

Oh.

Keira moved again, and this time she couldn't tell what was more noticeable—*his* heartbeat, or *hers.* Because she was definitely reacting to the way his skin felt under her hand, and the tightening of his arms didn't help, either. A lick of heat swept through her, and her light-headedness increased, too.

Focus on something else, she told herself. *Think of Mom and Dad. Think of work and the kids who need you. Think of Drew.*

But right that second, she couldn't even quite recall what Drew looked like. When she tried, his features blurred away, and the rugged looks of the unnamed Mountain Man overtook her mind instead.

Ugh.

Keira was *not* the kind of girl who rebounded from the idea of a marriage-potential relationship into the arms of a grunting, hulking man straight out of a hunting magazine.

Well. Not figuratively anyway.

Because she *was* quite literally wrapped in his firm grip, her head pressed into the crook of his arm.

Just how long had the Mountain Man been carrying her? And to where?

"Hey," she called, happy that her voice was a little louder.

But she still got no response. She tried again. "Mountain Man?"

He didn't slow.

"Hey!" This time, she said it as loudly as she could manage, and from the way his grip tightened on her, Keira was sure he'd heard her.

But he still didn't acknowledge her directly.

Stubborn.

With a great deal of effort, she wiggled an arm free from inside the jacket, snaked it out and yanked on his beard.

He drew in a sharp breath, snarled and released her. Keira tumbled to the ground. Hard.

Her back hit the snow, nearly knocking the wind out of her.

He looked down at her, regret in his gray eyes made visible by the moonlight behind him. Except then she opened her big fat mouth.

"You jerk! You dropped me!"

His expression tightened and he rolled his eyes.

Yeah, you think this is my *fault, don't you?* Keira thought. *Well, I didn't ask for the car accident. Or for the damned moose.*

"And I especially didn't ask for you and the stupid beard," she muttered.

He reached for her, concern evident on his face, and she shuffled backward along the snow.

"What?" Keira said with a head shake that made the world wobble. "You're worried about me because I don't want to be manhandled? I've got news for you. Non-forest-dwelling women have high expectations nowadays. No way are you getting those Sasquatch hands on me again. Not unless I ask you to."

She colored as she realized how that sounded.

And she strongly suspected that underneath that beard, he was trying to cover a sudden smile.

"Jerk," she muttered again.

He crossed his arms over his wide chest and gave her an expectant, eyes-narrowed glare. Silently daring her to stand up on her own.

"Yeah, I will," Keira snapped.

She pushed both hands to the ground and came to her feet. Rocks dug into her skin. Ice bit at her toes. And worse than that, her head was spinning again.

There was no way she was going to be able to walk more than a few feet. But there was also no way she was going to admit it to the smug Mountain Man.

And sure enough, his expression definitely said, *You need me.*

No way was she giving in to *that.* No matter how true it might be.

Keira straightened her body, grimacing as pain shot through her pretty much everywhere. In particular, her thigh burned, and she had to resist an urge to lift the jacket and have a closer look. Instead, she made herself meet the Mountain Man's stare.

"Where to?" she asked through gritted teeth.

He shrugged, then pointed to the black horizon.

"Great!" Keira said cheerily.

She had no idea what she was looking at. Or for. Vaguely, she thought again that she should probably ask him what he intended to do with her. But she was feeling rather stubborn, and the longer she was on her feet, the foggier her head was getting.

The Mountain Man stood still, watching her as she took two agonizing steps. He probably would've watched her take even more, except he didn't get a chance to. Because the world swayed, and Keira was unexpectedly on her rear end, staring up at the sky, transfixed by the few stars that managed to shine through the snowy sky.

Apparently, her little nap in the Mountain Man's arm hadn't done much of anything to renew her energy.

And now he was standing in front of her with that frown growing deeper with each heartbeat.

As he stared, Keira *did* begin to feel warm. But it had nothing to do with the weather or the accident, or anything at all that she could pinpoint.

Except maybe just...*him*.

Keira swallowed a sudden thickness in her throat and forced herself to look away.

Immediately she wished she hadn't, because the first thing that her eyes found was the fabric that had been wrapped around her thigh. When she'd struggled futilely to escape, it had slipped off and fallen into the snow. Keira frowned at it. It *had* been a light color, grayish or tan, it was hard to say which. But now it was dark.

Blood.

Instinctively, she knew that's what it was. And not just any blood. *Her* blood. Lots of it.

She brought her slightly floppy arm up so she could feel her leg.

Yep. It was damp and sticky. No wonder she

was so woozy. And no wonder the Mountain Man had been in such a hurry.

She sat there for a long second, then sighed in defeat.

"Hey, um, Mountain Man?"

He raised an eyebrow and looked down at her.

"So, yeah," she said. "I've decided we're not going to get very much farther if you stop carrying me."

His brow furrowed for one moment, then a wry chuckle escaped from his lips, and he plucked her from the ground as if she weighed nothing. But he only carried her for another minute. She looked at the run-down cabin that appeared before them. It screamed "horror movie."

They'd reached their destination.

Chapter Six

Graham could read Keira's expression perfectly as she looked from him to the wooden house.

Seriously? it said. *You're taking me in* there, *and you expect me to go without a fuss?*

If he'd felt inclined to speak, he would've replied, "Actually, I don't expect you to do anything without a fuss."

Instead he just shrugged, which made her emerald eyes narrow suspiciously. She went back to assessing the single-story structure with its rough shingle roof and its wide porch hung with ancient wind chimes. And likely found it lacking.

For the first time since he'd moved in semipermanently, he wished it was a more impressive abode.

The outside was purposefully left in disrepair, meant to deter anyone who saw it from wanting to enter.

He moved up the stairs, but as he reached the threshold, Keira's hand shot out, and Graham was too startled to realize what she was reaching for before it was too late. Her fingers closed on the well-worn sign. It was handcrafted by Graham's great-grandfather almost a century earlier when he'd built the cabin as a hunting outpost. Graham had meant to remove the handmade plate a long time ago.

"Calloway?" she said as she ran her fingers over the barely discernible lettering, then wriggled a bit so she could look at him. "That's you?"

She eyed him with patient curiosity, and a battle waged inside Graham's head. The last name wasn't an entirely common one, but it clearly hadn't sparked any recognition in her.

Given time, would she make the connection between him and the crime attached to the surname? If she did, would she simply chalk it up to coincidence, or would she investigate further?

In the end, Graham took a leap of faith and nodded tightly.

"Calloway," she repeated thoughtfully and added, "Is that a first name or last name?"

Graham tensed, but after a second, she smiled—the first genuine one Graham had seen since he found her—and he relaxed again. Her teeth were even, but not perfect, and the grin transformed her face. She went from porcelain perfection to devilish beauty.

"Or are you one of those people who just has the one name?" she teased. "Like the Cher of the survivalist world?"

Graham rolled his eyes, loosened one of his arms, tore the sign from its chain and tossed it with perfect aim into a wood bin on the porch. Then he carried her up to the door, turned the knob and let them into the cabin.

The heavy curtains ensured that it was almost dark inside, but Graham kept his modified woodstove on low, even when he wasn't in the cabin. As a result, the air was an ambient temperature. The only light—not much more than a dim glow—came from the same stove. At that moment, it highlighted the Spartan decor.

The furniture was limited to a set of rough-hewn chairs and a matching table, and Graham's own lumpy bed. He carted the girl across the room and deposited her on the latter. She tried to stand, but Graham pushed her back down and shot her a warning glare before he slipped to the other side of the room.

He wasn't doing anything else until he'd given her a more thorough look-over and tended to the mess of a wound on her leg.

Whether she likes it or not.

He dampened a clean cloth, then set some water to boil. He refused to think about anything but the immediate tasks at hand, and once he had the pot on the stove, he moved back to the bed.

As he seated himself beside her, she crossed her arms over her chest, and her mouth set in a frown. Graham ignored her expression, raising the cloth to her face. She snatched it from his hand.

"I can do it," she told him, but there was no bite in her words—just exhaustion.

Graham watched as she wiped away the grime left behind from sleeping in a hole and several hours of being carried through the woods. He was unreasonably pleased when she handed the cloth back and he saw that she only had the tiniest of abrasions on her otherwise perfect face.

Perfect face? Calm your raging manhood, Graham, he growled at himself. *It's clearly been far too long since you've seen a woman. And her prettiness is not your focus anyway. Her health is what's important. She needs to heal so you can get on with meeting up with Dave.*

He stood up stiffly, filled a tin mug with spices and pressed juice, topped it with the now-boiling water, then added a generous helping of his homemade booze. It wasn't as good as a painkiller or a sedative, but even if either had been available, he doubted she'd take one from him.

In moments, Graham was back at her side, offering her the steaming liquid. She eyed it suspiciously and didn't reach for it.

"I don't think so," she said.

Graham rolled his eyes, then grabbed the mug and took a pointed swig. Even the small mouthful warmed his throat as he swallowed.

He offered it to her again.

She still sniffed the drink, and Graham had to cover a smile.

"Fine," she muttered. "I guess you're not trying to poison me."

At last, she relented and took first one cautious sip, then another.

Satisfied that she was going to drink it, Graham slipped away again. He banged through the cupboards until he found each item he thought he might need and placed them on a tray. None of it was ideal—he didn't even seem to own a Band-Aid—but it would have to do.

Once he had everything ready, he opted to get changed. His clothes were dirty, and in some places soaked with the girl's blood. All of it risked contamination, and the last thing he wanted was to give her an infection.

Graham shot a quick glance in her direction. She was still engrossed in sipping the spiked drink, so Graham dropped his pants and stepped into a fresh pair of jeans instead. Then he stripped off his damp shirt and doused his hands and forearms with soap and some of the boiled water, then rinsed the suds off into a metal pot.

When he turned back to the girl again, the tin mug was at her side, and her eyes were fixed on him. They were wide, their striking shade of green dancing against the fairness of her skin. The orange firelight glinted off her hair, adding otherwise invisible hints of gold to the red.

Another bolt of electric attraction shot through Graham's blood.

Damn.

She really was beautiful.

Without meaning to, he let his gaze travel the length of her body. The white fur that had been covering her legs had slipped to the floor, leaving her calves bare. She still wore Graham's big, red jacket, but it didn't cover anything past midthigh. She tried to tug it down, but when one side lowered, the other rose, and after a second she gave up. It didn't help at all that he knew she had nothing but panties on underneath the coat.

Even from where Graham stood, he could see two spots of pink bloom in her cheeks. The added color in her fair skin did nothing to dampen his desire.

Double damn.

He forced himself to turn away and take a breath, rearranging the items on his tray until he was sure he could trust himself to get closer to her. He had to count to twenty to normalize his breathing, and even when he was done, he wasn't sure he was completely in control.

As he turned back, she looked as if she was bracing herself for an attack, and Graham couldn't say he blamed her. He felt unusually animalistic as he took careful, measured steps toward her. When he sat down, he made sure to leave a few inches between their knees.

Graham balanced the tray of makeshift first

aid supplies between them and took her horrified expression in stride.

He met her eyes and raised a questioning eyebrow.

"What? You're going to start requesting my permission *now*?" she asked.

Graham didn't cover his eye roll at all. He let her have it full force. Then he tipped the tray in her direction and waited as she inventoried the items there.

A white square of fabric he was going to use as a bandage. A mini airplane-serving size of vodka that would double as a disinfectant. A homemade, gelatinous salve Graham had created for treating the occasional burn. A punch-out package of antibiotics labelled Penicillin in bold letters and, finally, a hooked needle, threaded with fishing line.

Graham had to admit that the last thing glinted ominously in the dim light, but the rest was pretty innocuous.

Though clearly the girl didn't think so.

"Hell. No," she said.

She pushed the tray away and took a long pull of cider. Then she moved to set the mug down, but Graham closed his hand around hers, and he forced her fingers to stay wrapped around the handle. He tipped the mug to her lips. She swallowed the last of the cider, and he gave her an approving nod.

For one second, she looked offended.

But her eyes were already growing glassy and unfocused. Graham took the cup from her hands and placed it on the tray, opened the vodka, dabbed it onto the square of fabric and reached for the wound on her leg.

Keira batted at his hand, and when Graham frowned irritably, she just giggled and threaded her fingers through his. Startled, Graham didn't pull away immediately. Instead, he stared down, admiring the way her hand looked in his. Small and delicate. Soft and comfortable. In fact, it fit there. Just the way she'd fit in his lap.

"Hey…Mountain Man?"

Graham dragged his gaze up to hers. Her eyes were far too serious.

"You're not exactly my type," she said. "But if—*if*—I went for the angry, brooding hero kinda thing. I'd pick you." She paused, frowned a little, then added, "I don't think I meant to say that out loud. Am I *drunk*?"

She wobbled a little, almost slipping from the bed. Graham caught her. He eased her back onto the bed, smoothed back the mop of hair from her face and waited for her eyes to close.

Chapter Seven

Keira woke slowly, feeling slightly unwell.

Which should have alerted her to the fact that something was wrong even before she remembered where she was and how she got there.

She'd always been a morning person, awake and ready to go before the coffeepot finished brewing. When she'd lived at home with her parents, she and her dad got up at the crack of dawn. The two of them often watched the sun rise together. Then he would read the paper while she made breakfast for her mom, who would get up a solid hour after they did.

Keira valued those early hours, and when she'd finished her degree three years earlier and taken a job in social work, moving into her own place, she continued with the rise-before-dawn ritual.

So if she felt sluggish, as she did right at that moment, she was either hungover or seriously sick.

Which is it now? Keira wondered, somehow unable to recall quite what she'd been up to.

Then she pried her eyes open, and the sight of the cabin sent a surge of recollection and panic through her. A half a dozen thoughts accompanied the memory.

Calloway and his cider. Calloway, holding her hand, easing her back onto the bed.

And worse…Keira telling Calloway he wasn't her type.

Keira blushed furiously as she recalled the last few moments before she passed out. She'd been distracted by the way his palm felt over top of her hand. It was warm. Warmer even than the mug. And rough in a way she'd never experienced before. If she took the time to think about—which she now realized she hadn't—she supposed that Drew's hands were probably soft from the hours he spent sitting in an office and the occasional indulgence of a MANicure.

But not Calloway's. He had calluses on top of calluses, and Keira had had a sudden vision of him *actually* wielding an ax. Chopping wood for this very toasty fire. Topless. Because even in the snowy woods, that kind of manual labor worked up a serious sweat.

And there was no denying the potentially romantic ambience.

Secluded location. Check.

Tall, dark and handsome stranger. Check.

The gentle crackle of a fire. Check.

So maybe it wasn't that she *couldn't* recall what she'd been up to. Maybe it was that she hadn't *wanted* to remember it.

Clearly, what she needed was a minute to collect her thoughts and assess her surroundings. So she held very still and took stock of everything she could.

She was on her side, lying with her back pushed to the wall and her hands tucked under a pillow. She had a blanket wrapped around her, but there was an empty space beside her. The last bit made Keira swallow nervously. There was no denying that the spot was just the right size to hold a big, burly man.

Had he slept beside her?

Keira's face warmed again—both with embarrassment and irritation—at the thought.

Somehow, lying in the bed beside him seemed much more taboo than curling up beside him in a desperate attempt to keep warm postaccident in a snowstorm.

Still without moving, she scanned the limited area that she could see, hoping to find proof that she hadn't actually spent the whole night cuddled up next to Calloway. But it was a one-room deal—not huge, not small—with a table and chairs in one corner, and the still-burning woodstove in another. She supposed the bed where she lay was in a third corner. So, unless the fourth and final corner was home to a recliner or a second lumpy mattress, her fears were true.

She'd officially slept with the Mountain Man.

An inappropriate giggle almost escaped her lips as she pictured telling her best friend that she had no problem getting past the failed, so-called sign that was supposed to lead her to Drew. At all. She'd simply climbed into bed with the next man she met instead.

Keira knew her cheeks were still red, and she was glad Calloway wasn't there to see her reaction. If just the *idea* of sharing a bed with him made her feel so squirmy, actually confronting him about it would be a nightmare.

Where was he anyway?

"Calloway?" she called.

Keira wasn't expecting a spoken reply from the thus far mute man, but she did half anticipate his looming presence to step from some hidden alcove so he could stare down at her with that smirk on his face. But right that second, the cabin was completely silent. Which wasn't too terrible, considering the dull ache in her temple. The rest of her hurt, too, and she wondered if she needed medical attention beyond that of a serving of liquored-up cider, a questionable dose of penicillin and the makeshift care of a bona fide mountain man.

She pushed herself to a sitting position, and was pleased that her head didn't spin and that the ache eased off a little. But when she stood, her legs shook, and she realized she was still far weaker than she was used to. With a dejected sigh, she glanced around the room in search of something that would approximate a crutch. She spied a fire iron beside the stove, decided it would do and hobbled toward it.

Maybe there was something in the cabin itself that would answer her questions. She took another slow look around the single-room cabin.

Most of what she saw appeared to be pretty basic. The kitchen contained a wraparound cupboard, an ancient icebox and a rubber bin full of cast-iron pots.

She walked over and opened the icebox. It held the required slab of ice, several flat, wrapped packages that looked like steaks and—

"Beer?" Keira said out loud, surprised.

Calloway seemed more like the moonshine type than Bud Light. But there it was anyway. She closed the icebox and moved on to the cupboards. She didn't know what she thought she'd find, but it definitely wasn't instant hot chocolate and packaged macaroni and cheese. A bag of oatmeal cookies peeked out from behind a stack of canned soup.

So he wasn't that much of a survivalist after all.

As Keira let her gaze peruse the cabin a third time, she took note of some of the more modern accoutrements.

Sure, there was no television or microwave, but there was a dartboard and a current calendar and a digital alarm clock. A stainless-steel coffee mug sat on one windowsill, and a signed and mounted baseball adorned another.

For all intents and purposes, it was a middle-of-nowhere man cave. Minus the requisite electronics, of course.

Her curiosity grew.

Keira took a few more steps and banged

straight into a dusty cardboard box, knocking it and its contents to the ground.

Dammit.

She reached down to clean it up. And paused.

A notebook—no, a scrapbook—lay open on the floor. An ominous headline popped up from one of the newspaper clippings glued to its page.

Heiress and Son Gunned Down in Ruthless Slaying.

A gruesome crime scene was depicted in black-and-white below the caption, and Keira's fingers trembled as she reached for the book. She flipped backward a few pages.

Home Invasion Turns Deadly. And a photo of a tidy house on a wide lot.

She flipped forward.

Debt and Divorce. Police Close in on Suspect in Henderson Double Murder. A grainy shot of a short-haired man covering his face with the lapel of his suit jacket.

Something about the last headline struck Keira as familiar, and she frowned down at the page, trying to figure out if it was a case she'd heard about. She scanned the article. It was enticingly vague, just the kind of sensationalist journalism that baited the reader into buying the next edition. The suspect was listed as someone close to the victims and the words *unexpected twist* were used three times that she could see with just her quick perusal, making her think the "twist" was probably not "unexpected" at all, but that the reporter wanted to play it up anyway.

Then she clued in.

Derby Reach.

A chill rocked Keira's body. It wasn't just a familiar case. It was *the* case. The affluent community where she'd grown up, home to doctors, lawyers and judges—like her father—had been blown away by the double murder.

Keira remembered the day it occurred, but embarrassingly, not because of the tragedy itself. She'd met Drew that day. While the neighbors stood on their porches, gawking and gossiping, Drew had been walking through the street, totally clueless, as he searched for an open house he'd been booked in to view. She'd been the one to explain to him why no one was thinking about real estate at that moment. And his casual romantic pursuit of Keira started the moment he knocked on her parents' door by accident.

Now Keira wished she'd paid more attention to what was happening in her own backyard.

But why did Calloway have the scrapbook in his house? What connection could a man like him have with a wealthy socialite's death?

With the book still in her hands, Keira took a cautious, wobbly step back to the window.

Across the snowy yard stood Calloway. In spite of the subzero temperature, he hadn't bothered zipping up his coat. The wind kicked up for a second, tossing his thick hair and ruffling his beard. Calloway didn't seem to notice at all.

As Keira squinted through the glass, she frowned. A narrow figure in full protective gear—helmet, fur-lined hood, thick Gore-Tex pants and knee-high boots—stood facing Calloway, his hand resting on a parked snowmobile.

Something about the way the two men faced each other made Keira nervous. And as she tried to puzzle out the source of her distinct but unspecific unease, the wind changed and a loud voice carried in her direction.

"I've had a change of plans."

The breath Keira had been holding came out with a wheeze, and she stumbled back in surprise.

Calloway.

It was he who'd spoken.

Even though he'd turned so that his back was to her and he was blocking her view of the other man, Keira knew it was him. The deep, gravelly nature of the voice couldn't have suited him more perfectly.

Keira pressed her face almost right against the glass, and gasped again, this time not at Calloway. The other man had a gun, hooked menacingly to his side.

Keira took a step back. Her head spun. She needed to get away. From Calloway *and* his armed friend.

"My phone," she murmured, then looked toward the window again as she remembered.

It was in the pocket of the coat Calloway wore right that second.

Chapter Eight

The silence of the woods, combined with his habitual alertness, usually gave Graham plenty of notice whenever someone got even close to near to the cabin. More often than not, he could hear them for miles out.

This afternoon had been an exception.

A stupid exception, considering you knew *he was coming.*

But Graham had spent the whole night lying awake beside the girl, worrying about every pause in her inhales and exhales, overthinking every shift of her body, and second-guessing both his stitching job and his decision to ply her with the booze.

Was the fishing line too coarse to be effective? Were the stitches evenly spaced? Would the alcohol worsen the side effects of her concussion?

Graham had been so distracted by his concern that he didn't hear the approaching snowmobile until it was so close he could actually look outside and see it. He'd barely had time to close the door behind him before the man in front of him—who was currently struggling to unfasten his helmet—parked his vehicle at the edge of the house.

Graham worked at fixing something like a smile on his face.

As much as he trusted and relied on Dave Stark, he had a feeling that the girl's presence might jar the man's loyalty. It was one thing for the two of them to keep Graham's hideout a secret—adding an innocent unknown would be a whole different story.

So Graham stood with his hands in his jeans' pockets and waited with as much patience as he could muster for the familiar man to unclip and remove his helmet, and was careful to keep his

gaze forward. He didn't let his eyes flick wor-
riedly toward the cabin. Toward *her*.

The other man finally got his helmet free, and
when he whipped it off, Graham frowned. A
deep purple bruise darkened one of Stark's eyes,
and a long abrasion led from his left eyebrow to
the corner of his lip. He seemed indifferent to
the damage.

Graham gave the other man's appearance a
second, more scrutinizing once-over. Even aside
from his injuries, he did look unusually worse
for wear. His jacket was dirty and torn in a few
places. When he turned slightly, the cold sun
glinted off a metallic object at his waist.

A pistol.

Graham's eyes skimmed over it, then went
back to Dave's face. Never before had his friend
seen a need to bring a gun to the cabin. He
wasn't brandishing the weapon, but he wasn't
trying to disguise its presence, either. There was
something about the way he wore it that Graham didn't like.

"What the hell's going on?"

"I was about to ask you the same thing," Stark countered.

"Me? I'm not the one who looks like he just rolled out of a bar fight."

Dave shrugged. "Occupational hazard. You wanna tell me what you meant by 'change of plans'?"

"I meant that I'll make my own way into town."

Dave couldn't hide his surprise. Or the hint of fear in his eyes.

"Why would you do that?" he wanted to know.

"Few loose ends to tie up."

"Four years, we've been waiting for this. You've sunk every available penny into finding the man. What loose ends could possibly—" The other man cut himself off and narrowed his eyes shrewdly. "What's this about?"

Graham held his gaze steady. "I can't just walk away from this setup, Dave. If things go south with Mike Ferguson, I need to know that my space isn't in danger of being compromised."

Dave sighed. "It's *already* compromised."

"What do you mean?"

"Been an accident up on the road that comes in from the resort town," Dave replied. "Happened to catch it on the radio right before I left town. Car went over a cliff yesterday. Burned to a crisp. Couldn't even get a discernable VIN."

A dark chill crept up Graham's spine. "Not sure what a car accident's got to do with me. Or you, for that matter."

Dave's eyes strayed to the cabin. "You wanna rethink that?"

Graham refused to follow the other man's gaze. "Why? I've been up here four years and nothing has ever turned the radar my way."

"Is this how you want to play? Because if you can't trust *me*…"

It was Graham's turn to let out a breath. He trusted Dave about as much as he trusted anyone.

Which isn't much at all.

But there was no way he was admitting that. The man had been his best friend for two decades, and the only person he could count on for the past few of those.

"Explain it to me, then," Graham said instead. "Tell me how the accident affects me."

"I know cops, my friend. That radio chatter— it's suspicious. They think the burn was a little too perfect."

"So?"

"So, the only thing I know better than cops is *you*. And I know exactly what was going through your head yesterday when we talked on the radio. You were champing at the bit to get to Ferguson. I spent the whole day assuming you'd show up at the resort and that I'd have to hold you back. So I think maybe you *did* leave the cabin yesterday. And I think maybe something stopped you. Something that started out as a vehicle and ended up as a burned-up piece of trash."

"The road is forty miles from here. You think I could've trekked through that and made it back here already?"

Dave shook his head. "I don't think you took

the traditional route. The back way is only ten miles. Really rough terrain. But again…this is you we're talking about, isn't it? You've never done things the easy way."

Graham refused to take the bait. "The road is the last place I want to be. So I'm still not seeing what the accident has to do with me."

"It wasn't just a little crash. They're going to be looking for answers. And this isn't all that far to look. Come with me now. Unless you have some other reason for staying…"

As Dave trailed off, all the hair on the back of Graham's neck stood up.

"Get on your snowmobile, Dave," he replied, just short of a growl. "I'll come to you when I'm ready."

"C'mon, Graham—"

"*Now*, Dave."

"All right. This is your deal."

The other man slipped on his helmet, swung one leg over his snowmobile, then flipped up his protective visor and met Graham's cool stare.

"One other thing," he said. "She's a neighbor."

A neighbor? What the hell did that mean?

"She?"

"The driver."

"How could you even know the driver was a she?" Graham scoffed. "You said the car was burned to a crisp."

"It was. But I found *this* right alongside those snowshoe tracks."

Dave reached to the side of the snowmobile, unsnapped a storage compartment and pulled out a black purse, then tossed it through the air. Graham caught it easily. He didn't have to open it to know it was hers.

"Best guess, it'll take them two days to expand their search out this way," Dave added. "Tops. But that won't matter, right? Because you'll be on your way back home."

"Right," Graham agreed, hoping the word didn't sound as forced as it felt.

As Dave's vehicle disappeared into the snow, Graham's hand squeezed into a tight, angry fist, crushing the purse for a moment before he regained control.

Very slowly, he peeled his fingers from the purse. Even more slowly, he unsnapped it and opened the zipper. He reached straight for the wallet and slid out the driver's license. And there it was in black and white.

Keira London Niles. Resident of Derby Reach. The city where Graham had found Holly's broken body. What were the odds?

Slim to none.

Graham took three determined steps toward the cabin, then paused.

The front door creaked open, just a crack.

What the hell?

Graham took another cautious step. No way had he forgotten to close the door properly. He spun around just in time to see the girl—dressed in a pair of his boots and too-long sweatshirt— lift a metallic object behind her shoulder as if she was wielding a baseball bat. Her legs were more than a little shaky, but her face was set in a determined glare as she swung the fire iron straight at his chest.

Chapter Nine

The big man was too slick. As Keira swung with all her might, he leaned back like an action-movie hero, easily dodging the blow.

You might have overestimated your own abilities, too, she thought as she lost her footing and stumbled forward.

Keira shoved down the nagging voice. She preferred to blame it on him. Especially since he had his arms outstretched as if he was going to *catch* her of all things.

Ignoring him, she drew back the weapon again. And Calloway took a half a step back.

Good.

"Give me the coat," Keira commanded.

He frowned wordlessly, and Keira rolled her eyes.

"You can drop the silent, brooding stare," she said, just the slightest hint of a tremor in her voice. "I heard you talking to that other man. Who is he?"

Calloway gave her a long considering look before replying gruffly. "Drop the weapon and I'll drop the stare. Tell me what you heard."

For a moment, Keira went still as her brain caught up to her ears.

Calloway's voice had that same gravelly tinge she'd noted when it had carried on the wind into the cabin, only this close, it was amplified all the more. It was a good voice.

"I heard just enough to know you're a liar," she snapped. "Give me the coat and tell me who that man was."

He stared at her again, then shrugged and slipped the Gore-Tex from his shoulders.

"I don't know why you care," he told her. "And it's funny that you think *I'm* the deceptive one."

"What does *that* mean?" The defensive question slipped out before Keira could stop it, making her blush.

He held the jacket out. "It means I don't believe in coincidence."

"That makes two of us. Throw it."

Calloway tossed the jacket, and Keira caught it in the air, careful to keep one hand on the fire iron as she did it.

"I played all-star baseball in high school," she warned as she started to dig through the pockets in search of her phone. "And I once hit a home run with a broken arm. So don't assume that my injuries will make me any less willing to swing with everything I've got."

"I wouldn't dare."

Keira narrowed her eyes. She strongly suspected he was trying not to smile.

If he laughs, I'll hit him anyway, she decided. But he stayed silent.

Keira stuck her hand into another pocket. One she was sure she'd already explored. Where the hell was her phone?

"Are you looking for something in particular?" Calloway asked, his voice just a little too innocent.

She glared at him. "Listen. You might have saved my life—"

"Might have?" Graham interrupted. "You were unconscious. In a blizzard. I'm not sure *might* is the right word."

Keira's cheeks heated up. "I didn't mean it like that."

"So how did you mean it? The way *I* mean it when I say I might be standing outside, freezing, while a woman who I carried for ten miles, who I took into my house, who I gave my own *bed* to, aims a weapon at my head?"

The pink in Keira's face deepened to a cherry red, and he noticed her hand wavered. "I—"

Graham shook his head and cut her off again. "Or did you mean it like how I mean it when I say I might just be considering tossing you over my shoulder—again—carrying you *back* to the crash site and leaving you there?"

"You wouldn't!"

"I *might*."

His voice was dark, and Keira's eyes widened in surprise. She took a step back, her gaze no longer fixed on his face, but on his hand.

"That's my purse." She heard the tinge of fear in her statement.

"Keira London Niles of Derby Reach. There has to be a story in that name. Active member of Triple A. Twenty-four years old, just last month," he reeled off. "Happy birthday, by the way. Did you know your license was expired?"

"Give it back!"

He held it out, but there was no way for her to take it without losing her already tenuous hold on the fire iron in her hands.

"You don't want it anymore?" he asked.

"I'm not stupid," she grumbled.

"Far from it," Calloway agreed.

He set the purse down on the railing, reached into his pocket and pulled out a familiar black object. Keira felt the color drain from her cheeks, and the jacket slipped to the ground.

Well. That explains why I couldn't find it, she thought.

"Who were you going to call?" Calloway wondered out loud.

It was a good question. One Keira wasn't even sure of how to answer. Calling Drew seemed out of the question. Her parents were away on their annual European cruise. And her best friend would probably just laugh her butt off.

"The police," she whispered, not certain why she sounded so unsure.

Calloway tipped his head to one side, as if curious, and tapped the phone on his chin. "Not someone from *Derby Reach*?"

Why had he said it like that, with the tiny bit of emphasis on the name of her hometown? She recalled the scrapbook full of newspaper clippings about the murder in her hometown, and a little chill crept up her spine.

GRAHAM EXAMINED THE little crease between her brows, then the probing look in her emerald gaze. His gaze traveled down her face to her pursed lips. He almost believed the puzzled look to be genuine. And as a result, he also almost missed the subtle adjustment in her stance as she pulled an elbow back and prepared to strike.

I'm a sucker, he realized. *One pair of big green eyes, one bossy mouth, and I'm a mess.*

She swung and Graham ducked backward. He charged at her, and she lost her balance, stumbling toward the stairs. Automatically, Graham switched from an attack mode to defense mode. He reached out to stabilize her, and realized a moment too late her clumsiness had been an act, her near fall a feint.

Rookie mistake, he growled at himself.

She was already off at a run.

"What the hell!" Graham yelled after her.

She had to know she didn't stand a chance of getting away from him. Even if she hadn't been weakened by her injuries, Graham was at an advantage. His legs were longer, he was far more accustomed to the terrain than she was and he wasn't wearing boots five sizes too big.

Apparently, she wasn't going to let that stop her from trying.

Graham caught up with her just inside the tree

line on the edge of the clearing. His arms closed around her shoulders and the fire iron dropped to the ground. With a mutual grunt, the two of them fell straight into the snow.

She wriggled away, kicking viciously. Keira's foot met his chest, and when she drew it back for another round, Graham flung himself backward.

"Dammit!" he cursed as he landed hard on his rear end.

"Damn *you*!" Keira countered angrily.

She crawled along the snow, found a tree trunk and pulled herself up. But Graham was there in a flash.

"You can't win," he cajoled.

With desperation clear in her eyes, she charged at him. The surprise of the attack—more than the force of her body weight hitting him—knocked him to the ground once more. Graham let out another annoyed growl and sprung to his feet. By the time he was upright, Keira had the tire iron in her hands again, this time raised over her head.

"Stay back!" she yelled, and waved it around a little wildly.

Graham eyed the weapon dismissively, then focused on Keira instead. "Put it down."

"Fat chance."

"Put it down, or I'm going to *make* you put it down."

"I don't think so."

"Fine. Let's do things the hard way."

He stalked toward her, and with a cry, she tossed the fire iron at him, then turned and attempted to flee once more. She didn't make it more than four steps. Graham counted them. Then he slipped his arms around her slim waist and he lifted her easily from the ground.

Keira screamed, probably as loud and as long as she could, but her voice just echoed through the forest, bouncing back at her uselessly. She flung an elbow in the direction of Graham's stomach, but the attack didn't elicit more than a grunt. In a slick move, he flipped her around and pinned her to a large evergreen, then fixed his eyes on hers.

Keira continued to struggle, but Graham wasn't even pretending to let her get away. She finally seemed to give in, and she stopped fighting. She slid to the ground, but he continued to hold her arms as he glared down at her. Her breath was coming in short gasps and her limbs were shaking.

On the ground, she looked small and fragile once more.

For a second, Graham felt guilty. He'd made himself responsible for her well-being. Taken her in to care for her. Yeah, she'd lashed out at him for some reason he couldn't understand. But she was probably scared as hell and still shaken up. And maybe her hometown *was* just a coincidence after all.

Graham loosened his hold, just slightly. Then she attempted to twist away, and guilt evaporated. He squeezed her wrists together over her head, pressed a foot—as gently as he could while still being firm—into *her* feet and immobilized her.

"I'm done playing games," he told her in a low voice.

She lifted her chin defiantly. "What are you going to do? Kill me?"

Her question hit him hard, square in the chest. She *did* know him. Or thought she did.

No coincidences.

"I'm not a murderer," Graham replied coldly, and dropped her wrists. "And what I'm going to *do* is take you back inside. Where we're going to eat breakfast like two normal adults. And where you're going to tell me exactly what the hell you were doing up this mountain in the first place. Understood?"

She nodded meekly, and Graham had to shove down the reflexive regret at dampening the fire in her eyes.

You need answers, he reminded himself.

He pulled back, and as he did, Keira tipped up her head. The new angle gave him a perfect view of her eyes, and Graham saw with relieved satisfaction that the fire—quite clearly—wasn't extinguished. Just banked.

Chapter Ten

As Calloway's seemingly enormous body eased away from Keira's own petite one, she realized how ridiculous it was to think she could have overpowered him in the first place. The self-defense training she received at work was no match for his brute strength. No makeshift weapon would outdo him.

"Let's go," he said.

Even if his voice hadn't demanded obedience, he didn't release her, and that gave her little choice but to go where he propelled her. They moved toward the cabin, Graham's hands pressed firmly into Keira's shoulders, her feet dragging a little in the oversize boots.

Stupid, stupid, she cursed herself as they moved along. *I would've been better off taking my chances by running into the woods instead of thinking he owed me some kind of explanation.*

Because he really *didn't* owe her one. And if Keira thought about it, she was probably the one who owed *him* something. Had she even thanked him for saving her? She couldn't remember. She opened her mouth to do it now, then paused as she second-guessed the impulse. Should she still thank him now that she suspected he had something to do with the four-year-old homicide in her hometown?

I'm not a murderer, he'd said.

Did that make it true? Keira desperately wanted to believe him. And not just because she was trapped on the mountainside with him, and her only way out—so far—was a man with a snowmobile and a gun. Something about Calloway felt intoxicatingly *right*. Especially when he was standing as close to her as he was now, his hand on her body, guiding her where he wanted to go.

When they moved up the stairs, and he reached around her to push open door, his clean, woodsy scent assaulted her senses, rendering her brain temporarily nonfunctional. Her booted toe caught on the transition board at the bottom on the door frame, and before she could stop herself, she was falling forward. She braced herself to hit the ground. But the impact didn't come.

She still fell, but not the way she'd been thinking she would. One of Calloway's arms slipped under her legs, and the other closed around her shoulders. As she went down, he took the full force of the ground to his own elbows and knees. He had one hand on the back of her neck, the other on her thigh, and his gray eyes held her where she was.

They were both breathing heavily, and Keira refused to acknowledge the treacherous parts of her body that demanded to know why it felt so good to be looking into one another's eyes, chests rising and falling in near unison.

A drop of water fell from his face to hers, and he eased his hand out from behind her hair to wipe it away gently. His fingers burned pleasantly against her skin, and it didn't help at all when he looked her straight in the eyes and gave her the clearest understanding of the term *white-hot* that she'd ever had. It was the perfect way to describe the way ice gray met fierce need in Calloway's eyes. They were burning so bright, she almost had to look away. But couldn't.

Lying above her, looking at her like that, Calloway wasn't just handsome. He was gorgeous. The perfectly rustic look had basically turned him into the supermodel version of his Mountain Man self.

And, oh, he smelled good, too. Even better than he had when he was carrying her up the mountainside. Raw and woodsy and tinged with smoke.

He was unpredictable and dangerous, and it was totally unreasonable to be this attracted to him. The smart part of her brain knew it. But the smart part didn't seem to be attached to the rest of her. In fact, there were a few distinct bits that seemed *remarkably* detached from her brain altogether.

Keira's whole body was alight.

Kiss me, she begged silently.

And as her heavy gaze continued to hold Calloway's, she knew he was going to.

Thank God.

Then, so slowly she was sure he was very carefully gauging her reaction, he slid his hand from her cheek to her chin and tipped it toward him. He inched forward. Keira fought an urge to speed it up, to drive her lips into his, to close the miniscule gap between them and take what she was dying to have. What she suddenly realized she'd been dying to have since the second he put his arms around her in the snowstorm.

Don't rush this, whispered a small voice in her head.

And Kiera suspected that the voice was right. This kiss—this first kiss with such an intense, unusual and mysterious man—was something to be savored.

His mouth touched hers, his eyes still wide-open.

It was the softest kiss. The gentlest one. But

it ignited more passion in Keira than she'd felt in her entire quarter-of-a-century-long life. She gasped because she couldn't help it. She closed her eyes because she had to. And when Calloway's palm skidded to the back of her neck again, her arms came up, all on their own, to encircle his waist. She pulled him close, and he let her. The aches in her body eased away as she let the rest of the kiss take her, as his lips became hungry, and everything but Calloway faded to the background.

But it was painfully short.

He pulled away, ending the embrace with an abruptness that contrasted sharply with its slow beginnings.

It left Keira full of longing.

"Calloway," she whispered.

He leaned in once more, grazing her mouth, and then—without warning—he abandoned his pursuit of her lips to swoop in and lift her up instead. He carried her straight to the bed, and for a dizzying moment Keira thought he was going to skip the preamble and go straight for the main attraction.

Quicker than she could decide whether or not she should protest, he reached beneath the frame, grabbed a rope, wrapped it around her wrists tightly and secured her to the bed.

DAMMIT.

Complications were low on Graham's list of priorities. Liking Keira Niles was *very* complicated.

And he did like her. Even before they'd shared the most intense kiss he'd ever experienced.

He liked that she was wearing his clothes. He liked the way the lithe muscles in her thighs disappeared under his shirt, hinting at what lay farther up. He even liked the way she was glaring at him right that second, mad instead of scared, a hint of residual passion evident in the way her lips stayed slightly parted and the way her gaze kept flicking between his eyes and his own mouth.

Beautiful, resilient, strong and smart.

His *like* was making it hard to see her as a threat, and he really needed to overcome that. Somehow.

"What do you think you're doing?" she snapped.

"Did you know I was here?" he replied softly, ignoring her angry question. "Or did you just get lucky?"

"I wouldn't call this lucky."

Keira pulled emphatically on the rope around her arms, and Graham winced. Coercion didn't suit him, and in spite of what people thought, he wasn't a violent man. Not habitually anyway. He just did what he had to do, when he had to do it.

"If you're not going to answer my questions," Graham said, "then I'm going to go back to our previous arrangement."

"What previous arrangement was that?" she replied, just shy of sarcastic.

"The one where I don't speak at all."

He started to turn away, but she snorted, and he stopped, midturn, to face her again.

"More of the silent treatment? What are you?" she asked. "A ten-year-old boy?"

For some reason, the question annoyed him far more than her lack of candor. Graham strode toward her, and once again she didn't cower. She raised her eyes and opened her mouth, but whatever snarky comment had been about to roll off her tongue was cut off as Graham mashed lips into hers. Uncontrollably. He kept going until he'd possessed her mouth completely, and when it ended, Keira was left gasping for air—gasping for *more*. For good measure, he dug his hands into the hair at the back of her neck and trailed his lips from her chin to her collarbone before he stopped.

"When you're ready to talk—with some honesty—I'll be just over there, waiting," Graham growled against Keira's throat.

Then he stood and moved across the room to dig out the things he needed to prepare breakfast.

Just a morning like any other, he told himself.

Except that he needed two plates and two forks instead of the usual one of each. And twice the amount of pancake batter and extra coffee. Oh, and there was also the faint feminine perfume that somehow managed to override the scent of fire that usually dominated the air in the cabin. Those things, coupled with the way her heated gaze followed each of his movements while he stoically ignored her presence, left no doubt that the morning wasn't *any*thing like any other.

Why couldn't he have rescued a hideous beast of woman with no spark in her whatsoever? Why did it have to be a girl who so thoroughly piqued his interest and so easily distracted him from finding Mike Ferguson? He should be trying to think of a way to get her out of his house as quickly as possible so he could get back to his mission. Not standing there daydreaming about her. He could barely blink without seeing her enticing form on the back of his eyelids.

"If I answer your questions, will you answer mine?"

Keira's voice startled Graham, and he spun toward her. The pan went slack in his grip, and the golden breakfast item flew right past both it and him, and landed on the floor at his feet.

They both stared at it for a moment before Graham bent to snatch it up.

"Well?" Keira prodded.

Graham shrugged. "Depends."

She blinked, looking surprised. Had she just expected him to agree with no further terms? Not a chance in hell was he giving her the freedom to ask anything she felt like.

"It depends on what?" she asked.

Graham took a breath, popped the floor pancake into his mouth, then chewed it slowly and deliberately before swallowing it and answering her puzzled question. "On whether or not I think you're telling the truth. And whether or not I think giving *you* an honest answer will put you in danger."

"Shouldn't I be the one who decides if I'm in danger?" she countered.

Damn, he liked her stubbornness. He ran his fingers over his beard to cover his smile.

"Not today," he told her.

"Listen to me, Mountain Man. You might have saved my life—" Keira paused when Graham raised an eyebrow, and quickly amended, "You *did* save my life. But you also lulled me into a drunken stupor with your liquored-up cider, then crawled into bed with me, and now you've tied me up, and—"

He cut her off. "I also stripped you down, searched your body for signs of any other deep cuts or contusions, or internal bleeding. Then I stitched you up as best I could."

With each word, Keira's face grew redder, and by the end of Graham's speech, she was nearly purple.

"You *stripped* me?" she asked, her voice a squeak. "Why would you *strip* me? And then *tell* me about it?"

Graham shrugged. "I thought it best that I get that out of the way now. And it would've been hard to be thorough if you'd been clothed. That's two questions you owe me now, by the way."

"I don't owe you anything," she almost yelled. "You cannot touch me or kiss me, just because you feel like it. You cannot carry me around, just because it's easier than asking me nicely."

"You think I did all that for *me*?" Graham argued.

"I'm sure it was horribly inconvenient for you to get me naked."

Graham bit back an admission that it *had* actually been damned inconvenient. He'd covered her body carefully while searching for anything more serious than the slice in her thigh. For the first time in his life, he'd been barely able to keep his professional detachment in place, and the guilt of it had made him want to perform the careful examination of her body with his eyes closed. Except the thought of a hands-only exploration brought with it a whole host of other, far from clinical, ideas to mind. He had never been so happy to finish an exam.

Now he was sorry he'd brought it up.

"You were asleep," he growled.

"And sleep made me what? Unwomanly? Unattractive?"

Hell. No.

"High on yourself, aren't you?" Graham asked, his voice just a little too dark to be called teasing.

"What does that mean?"

"You clearly think your nudity is enough to turn a man into nothing more than a slobbering sex-crazed maniac," he stated.

"That's not what I said!"

"That's what I heard."

Keira's face was still pink. "It's just that that stuff makes it a little hard to trust that you've got my best interests at heart."

He *had* done all of those things she'd mentioned. He'd also covered her each time she kicked off her blankets in the night, panicked each time her breathing changed and had his own night thoroughly ruined.

Ruined? he thought. *Or made more worthwhile.*

He growled at the voice in his head and pushed it away.

"You're welcome," Graham said.

"You're—I'm—what?"

Ignoring her incomprehensible, sputtering reply, Graham walked over to Keira and unfastened the rope. Then, in a quick move that made her squeak, he scooped her from the bed, carried her over to the little table and secured her to one of the chairs.

"I'll let those first two questions go, and even let you ask another. In the name of chivalry," he said, and raised an eyebrow expectantly.

Chapter Eleven

If her hands hadn't been tied together, Keira would've crossed her arms over her chest in indignant frustration.

"You think you're chivalrous?" she demanded.

The big man grinned smugly. "Yes."

"You may want to buy a dictionary."

"Either way…it's my turn. You've asked three questions, and I've asked none."

"I haven't even asked my *first* question yet!" Keira protested. "And you said you were going to let the first two go."

"Changed my mind. My house, my rules," he replied.

"You are an infuriating man."

He nodded. "I'm also loyal, thorough, a tad controlling and a damned fine cook. Are you hungry?"

"Is that *your* question?"

"As a matter of fact…it is."

Keira rolled her eyes. "No, I'm not hungry."

"First question and already you're telling me a lie," Calloway said and he pushed a plate of pancakes toward her.

She shoved it back. "It's not a lie."

Calloway gripped his fingers on the edge of the plate and pushed it across the table. When it reached Keira, she tried to send it back again, but he didn't let it go.

"I'm not going to eat just because you tell me to," she informed him.

In reply, he dragged the pancake away.

Ha, Keira thought triumphantly. *Take that.*

But he wasn't letting her win. He was just upping his game. He smiled and began to cut the pancake into bite-size pieces. Then he scraped his chair over the floor so that he was right beside her. He jabbed a fork into one of the pieces and held it up to Keira's mouth.

It smelled damned good.

She turned her head away anyway.

Calloway exhaled, clearly frustrated.

Keira tipped her face back in his direction, prepared to snap something mean and clever at him. But the second she opened her mouth, his fingers were there. A piece of pancake slipped into her mouth, and it was syrupy and sweet and so soft it practically melted away when it hit her tongue.

Oh, my God.

It was the best pancake Keira had ever tasted. Maybe the best *food* she'd ever tasted. All thoughts of ropes versus chivalry went out of her head. When Calloway lifted another piece from the plate, there was no hope in hell she was turning it down. She opened her mouth eagerly, and he popped it in. Keira couldn't even act embarrassed as her mouth closed quickly and she nipped his fingers. It really was that good.

A little noise—just barely shy of a *yum*—escaped from her lips as she swallowed.

Calloway raised an eyebrow.

"Fine," Keira relented. "I take back the breakfast thing. But on the other one, I stand firm. No touching."

He smiled as if he didn't believe her, lifted another piece of pancake from the plate, raised an eyebrow and held it out. After the briefest hesitation, Keira opened her mouth, and Calloway popped it in. He let out a deep laugh, and the fourth piece he offered to her a little more slowly. When Keira parted her lips eagerly, he drew the pancake away.

"Hey!" she protested.

Graham leaned his elbows on the table. "You ready to answer another question? Truthfully, this time?"

"I wasn't *lying*," Keira argued. "I just didn't know I was hungry."

"Uh-huh."

"Besides which. I'm pretty sure it's *my* turn to ask a question."

"We both know that's not true," Calloway said, and grinned again.

He held the pancake positioned between his thumb and forefinger, just out of biting distance. Keira bent forward to grab it. This time, when he tried to tease her, she jerked her bound hands up, and just barely managed to get enough slack that she could close them on his forearm.

Calloway chuckled, but he let her take the pancake. She made an exaggerated *mmm* noise as she sucked it back, not realizing that she wasn't nibbling on just the pancake. Calloway's fingers were still sandwiched between her lips, pleasantly smooth and soft on his calloused skin. Heat shot through her, and when she relaxed her jaw to release his fingers, he didn't pull away. Instead, he swiped his thumb over the corner of her mouth, collecting a drop of syrup. Then he pushed it back to the tip of her tongue, and Keira gave his thumb a little lick, relieving it of the wayward syrup.

"Thank you," she said softly. "For helping me and fixing me up."

"Anytime."

There was a weight behind his tone that didn't match the typically dismissive expression. As if he meant it literally.

Anytime.

Keira's pulse raced, and her heart swelled pleasantly at the thought that Calloway would drop everything just to help her. That maybe he had *already* dropped everything to help her.

In the soft, wintry sunlight filtering through the cabin, there was no mistaking the want in his eyes. A matching one flowed through Keira.

Slowly, he loosened the rope on her wrists. And when she was free, she didn't make a run for it. Instead, she let him twine their fingers together, then lift their joined hands to her cheekbone. He ran them across her skin. She leaned closer. Her mouth was so near to his that she could already almost taste him.

At every turn, she wanted him more and cared less about what had brought her there in the first place. Two more seconds of his knee pressed between hers under the table, and she was going to be insisting that he take her back to that lumpy bed in the corner.

"You okay?" he asked.

The question threw her a little.

"Am I okay?"

His shoulders went up and down. "Give me a sliding scale? One through ten."

He really did sound serious.

"My head aches. So three out of ten for that. You untied me, so five out of ten for that. And I'm not dead. So I'll concede a ten out of ten for that."

"So...an overall of about six out of ten. Sixty percent isn't too bad."

"It's not exactly A material."

"Maybe you could bump it up to a C+ if I lent you some pants?"

The burn of desire, just under Keira's skin, came back, full force. Her legs *were* bare. And they were wrapped around one of Calloway's denim-clad ones. Put that together with the way his beard was close enough to tickle, the deep rumble of his voice making her chest vibrate,

and Keira knew she was in a completely different kind of trouble. One that had nothing to do
with Calloway's secrets or the armed man with
whom he was acquainted. That stuff—that dangerous stuff—seemed ridiculously far away at
the moment.

But she needed to remember it. And to do *that*,
she needed space. Reluctantly, she pulled away.

Forcing a measured tone, Keira whispered,
"Pants don't outweigh the left-me-tied-to-a-bed,
rifled-through-my-purse creep factor. Can I ask
my question now?"

"Can you…" Calloway trailed off, looking at
her as though he couldn't quite understand the
request.

Then he cleared his throat and shoved back
his chair, irritation making his eyes flash as he
stood up and yanked away the nearly empty pancake plate.

Guilt tickled at Keira's mind, but she pushed
it down.

"Can I ask my question?" she repeated.

With a coolness that didn't match the burn of

his gaze, Calloway replied, "I think you're still in the red, as far as questions are concerned."

He crossed his arms and glared down at her.

Refusing to be intimidated, Keira jumped to her own feet and opened her mouth to argue, but an abrupt wave of dizziness made her head spin.

Immediately, Calloway seemed to sense the change. His eyes filled with concern. And then his hands were on her, easing her close with a gentleness that contrasted dramatically with his bulky form. He lifted her from the ground and cradled her to his wide chest.

Right away, Keira felt better. Sleepy, but better. Almost content.

He brushed her hair back from her forehead, letting his palm rest there for an extra second.

"Overdid it," he murmured.

His apologetic tone made Keira want to absolve him of responsibility. It had been her careless disregard for that weather that had led to the accident. Her attempt to come after Calloway with the fire iron that made her arms ache.

But she couldn't form the words.

After a moment, she gave up trying and pushed her face into the soothing firmness of his body instead. She could hear his heart. It was beating loudly, and she liked its steadiness. Appreciated its strength. Appreciated *his* strength.

A little sigh escaped Keira's lips as she let both him and his heartbeat surround her.

As Calloway moved across the floor, she noted that his pace matched the thumps. And in a light-headed way, she wondered if the blood rushing through her was going to match it soon, too.

But in a few steps, he reached the bed, drew back the blankets and laid her down, and Keira realized she wasn't going to get a chance to find out.

Regret made her heart ache.

Why was I arguing with him?

Keira couldn't remember.

Using the last bit of her strength, she reached for him.

"Stay," she managed to whisper.

Keira knew the muddled way her head felt was what made her say it. Or what *let* her say it.

But she didn't care.

He met her eyes, and some undefinable emotion brimmed over in their silvery stare, and he peeled back the blanket and slid into the bed, and Keira didn't just not *care* that reason had slipped away...she was glad.

GRAHAM WOKE ABRUPTLY, inhaled deeply, then froze as Keira's scent filled him.

What the...

Then he remembered. She'd looked up at him with those half-closed eyes, issued the one-word plea, and he'd been unable to do anything but indulge her, crawling in beside her and cradling her close until she was sound asleep.

She wasn't the only one being indulged. You could've at least tried to resist. Would have, if you really wanted to.

That was the truth.

He could use whatever excuse came to mind—checking her breathing, making sure she was just exhausted and not injured further or feverish—but when it came down to it, Graham simply wanted her close.

Not just close...in your bed.

He couldn't even remember the last time he'd even *thought* about taking a girl to bed.

Somewhere between four years and never again.

Or longer.

Because even before your life fell apart, things on that front were less than satisfying.

Graham ran his fingers through a loose strand of Keira's hair and watched her eyelids flutter. He sure as hell didn't lack desire right that second. Or any second since she'd appeared out of thin air. In fact, his desire for this girl seemed more central to his life than any other thing.

Keira shifted a little beside him, and her slim fingers found his shirt. She tightened her grip on the fabric for a moment, and then she stilled again. As if she'd just been making sure he was still there. Graham's heart squeezed a little in his chest before he could stop it.

Stupid.

Very carefully, he put his hand over hers and loosened her hold on his clothes, then eased out of bed.

As silently as he could, he slipped on his favorite plaid jacket, then let himself out onto the porch.

Graham was startled to see that the sun had dipped down behind the mountain and that dusk was already settling in. He'd done none of his usual chores, performed none of the ritualistic tasks that had occupied him for the past four years. No perimeter scan, no check to make sure everything was ready to go should he have to leave suddenly, nothing. He'd somehow slept the day away. With Keira London Niles.

Graham took a deep breath, trying to clear the thoughts in his head and her delicate aroma out of his nostrils. The inhale of cool air helped with the second, but did nothing at all in regard to the first.

He fought to keep from heading straight back inside, then tightened his jacket and shoved aside a pile of snow so that he could slump down onto the rarely used porch rocker. The wood underneath him was icy enough to creep through his jeans, but Graham continued to sit there anyway. It seemed like a suitable punishment for the heat that stirred in him each time his mind drifted toward Keira.

Dammit.

He couldn't afford to be feeling like this about a girl he barely knew.

Hell. He couldn't allow himself to have feelings at all. His soft side was what got him into this mess in the first place.

What *was* she doing there? Was she telling the truth about not knowing Graham was on the mountain?

The second she was well enough, he was going to demand answers. Not because he wanted to, but because he had to. To protect himself, and more important, to protect her.

Graham's chest constricted again as he thought of how dangerous it was for Keira to be there with him. She couldn't have picked a worse savior. Even just knowing his name was enough to pull unnecessary, unwanted attention her way. If she repeated it, the authorities would descend on her.

Or worse.

Mike Ferguson might come looking.

Graham needed to ensure that didn't happen. More than he needed anything else. And sitting around thinking about that didn't help any more than lying in bed beside her did.

He started to stand, but only got as far as putting one hand on the arm of the rocker.

Keira was up. Awake. Standing in the doorway. Even though she'd draped a blanket around her shoulders, Graham could see that she'd taken the time to get dressed in one of his T-shirts and a pair of his sweats—cinched tight, but still hanging off her hips. She looked sleepy and sexy and about as perfect as one person could.

Graham stared for a long second, mesmerized by the way the waning light brought out the creamy tone of her skin and deepened the auburn in her hair.

He took a breath, then wished he hadn't because her sweetness was in his nose once again. He did his best to ignore it and forced himself to speak.

"You shouldn't be up," he greeted gruffly.

"Morning to you, too, Mountain Man," she replied.

Graham's eyes flicked to the moonlit sky.

"Evening," he corrected.

"Always have to have the upper hand, don't you?"

He gave her a considering look, wondering how she could possibly believe he had the upper hand. Just looking at her made him feel…not exactly helpless. Not exactly powerless.

Spellbound, maybe.

"You should go back inside," Graham said, deflecting her question so that he wouldn't have to admit just how out of his element he felt right then.

In reply, she narrowed her eyes in the already-familiar way that told him she wasn't interested in doing what he thought she ought to do.

With the same stubborn look on her face, Keira moved toward him instead of away from him.

Graham opened his mouth to point out that she might not like the way things turned out if she did as she wanted instead of as she should, but he didn't have to say a word. Right before she reached the porch swing, the slippery ground did it on his behalf.

Keira's feet, which were dwarfed inside a pair of his socks, skidded along the ice and with an "Oomph," she landed in his lap.

She made as if she was going to get up, but Graham wasn't going to let her go so easily; she felt far too good, right there in his lap.

"Stay."

He realized immediately that he'd echoed her earlier request—the one he hadn't been able to deny—wondered if she noticed it, too. If she did, she didn't say.

But after a minute, she leaned against him and tucked her feet up. Automatically, Graham's arms came up to pull her even closer. It was strange, how natural it felt to hold her like that.

"At least this way, I know you're not freezing your rear end off," he said into the top of her head.

There was a tiny pause before she asked, "Is that why you want me to stay?"

"No," Graham admitted.

"But you're still not going to tell me anything, are you?" she replied.

He ran his hands over her shoulders, then down her arms and rested his palms on her wrists.

"No," he said again. "Not because I don't want to."

"What's stopping you?"

"My gut."

"Your gut tells you not to trust me?"

Graham chuckled. "Actually, my gut tells me that I *should* trust you."

Graham moved his hands from her wrists to her hands and threaded his fingers through hers.

He suddenly found himself wondering if *she* trusted *him*. What *her* gut had to say.

Maybe she hadn't even considered it.

Did he want her to?

She really shouldn't trust him. His past was too troublesome, his heart too marred. He might hurt her in his attempt to keep her safe. Hell, he had nothing to even offer. Not until he'd taken care of Mike Ferguson and all that went along with finding the man.

But he wanted her faith, and not blindly. He wanted to know that he hadn't lost the quality that made a girl like Keira believe in him.

"So…" she prodded after his long moment of silence.

Graham jerked back to the present moment. "My gut tells me to trust you. But it's warning me even louder that if I tell you my story, it'll put your life at risk."

"Isn't that my risk to take?"

"It should be, yes," he agreed.

"But not now?"

"I didn't save your life just to let you get killed, Keira."

Her hands tightened on Graham's. "Are you sorry?"

"Sorry about what?"

"That you saved me."

The quiet, trying-not-to-sound-hurt voice cut into Graham's chest. He couldn't stand the thought of her believing that.

He released her hands so he could reposition her, so he could see her face and she could see his.

"No matter what happens, Keira," he stated softly, "I'll never be sorry that I saved you."

A little smile turned up the corners of her so-kissable lips, and Graham wanted to make it even wider.

"I'll tell you what," he said. "If you come inside and let me feed you dinner *and* you manage to stay awake for more than five minutes after, I'll answer one question. Your way."

"Carte blanche?"

That smile of hers reached her eyes.

In spite of his head screaming at him *not* to say yes, Graham couldn't help but give in.

"If you promise not to ask me anything too terrible during dinner, then yes."

"What do you want? Small talk?"

Graham nodded. "Small talk. In exchange for carte blanche."

And her full lips widened into a grin, and that spellbound feeling slammed into Graham's heart once more.

Chapter Twelve

True to his word, Calloway kept the conversation light. He fed the woodstove and heated up some thick soup and told her he hadn't seen so much snow in the mountains in a long time. With a head shake, he deflected her question about precisely how long.

And in spite of her resolve to stay awake, and her nearly daylong nap, the second she finished her soup Keira could feel her eyes wanting to close and sense her mind wandering. She tried to keep it focused. But when she pushed her bowl away, a yawn came out instead of a question.

If she did manage to stay awake...what would she ask?

Just a few hours ago, she swore that she had a dozen all-important, totally articulate things she *had* to know about who Calloway was and what he was doing there on the mountain. About his interaction with the man outside. About the box of newspaper clippings.

Now all the specifics were muddled.

"Keira?"

His voice, rumbling with amusement, made her jerk her head up from its unintentional resting place on her hand.

Calloway had cracked one of the beers from the fridge and looked far more relaxed than Keira expected.

He looks so...normal.

Which was somehow comforting. A beer and a fire and cozy evening. Keira wished wistfully that it could be that simple.

"You awake?" he asked.

"Yes," she lied.

Clearly, she'd drifted off enough to give him time to get the beer from the fridge. Funny that she was already so comfortable with this man—

complete with all his dangerous edges—after such a short time. And not a single alarm bell was going off, either.

Calloway took a swig of his beer and gave her a considering look that matched her own. "So. Does this mean you have something to ask me?"

Keira tried again to recall what, specifically. She'd had something in mind. It eluded her now.

"Did you feed me soup to make me sleepy?" She wanted to know.

A grin broke out on Calloway's face. "I give you carte blanche and that's the question you choose?"

"You know perfectly well that wasn't it at all." Another yawn took away from the emphatic way she meant to make the statement.

"Why don't you lie down while you think about it?" he suggested.

"Nice try."

Calloway's smile widened. "I could carry you over to the bed again."

"You'd like that, wouldn't you?"

"Maybe I would."

His eyes did a slow head-to-toe inventory of Keira's body. They rested on each part of her just long enough to make the object of his attention warm, then moved on to the next.

Feet and ankles. Knees and thighs. Hips and waist. The swell of her breasts.

He paused at her lips and lingered there before he raised his gaze up again, and then he came to his feet and began to clear their table.

And even though Calloway had broken the stare and his eyes were otherwise occupied, Keira knew there was no *maybe* about it.

He would enjoy taking her to bed.

And if Keira was being honest, she craved the closeness, too. She wanted the feel of his arms around her and she wanted to taste his lips again.

Maybe the heated desire she felt was amplified by her surroundings, maybe it was made more intense by how close she'd come to death just yesterday.

Probably.

It made sense psychologically—reasonably.

Her training in the social work field had taught enough about transference.

But underneath that, Keira felt a stronger pull.

He'd rescued her, at the risk of his own safety. And he was still putting her life ahead of his own.

A man like that...he deserved appreciation.

Appreciation. Yeah, that's *what you feel.*

She shoved aside the snarky thought and watched Calloway rinse their bowls, then dry them.

His body moved smoothly and confidently, un-daunted by the stereotypically feminine activity. Keira liked the glimpse of domesticity. A lot.

"Keira?"

She jumped in her seat. "Yes?"

"Nothing. Just checking."

"Checking what?"

"Whether you'd fallen asleep or whether you were staring at my rear end."

"Very funny."

Calloway chuckled. "It was the only reason I

could think of for you *not* offering to dry while I washed."

Keira's face warmed, and she stood up quickly. But the big man was at her side in a second, his hand on her elbow.

"Hey," he said. "I was kidding. You need to rest, not do dishes."

"I've rested an awful lot already."

"Not enough."

Warmth crept from his palm into her arm and through her chest, and she couldn't argue as he led her across the room to the bed. And she felt a little lost as he released her.

Definitely more than transference.

She looked up at his face, wondering how she'd ever questioned whether or not he was handsome. He was near perfect.

"In my other life," he told her, his voice low, "it was my job to take care of people. I want you to get better, Keira. Soon. So all I need right now is to make sure you're all right."

He pulled up the blanket from the bed, tucked it around her face, then cupped her cheek. And that second, Keira remembered what he'd said about his gut and trust, and something clicked home for her.

"I work for child protective services," she said slowly, "and I have to form snap judgments sometimes. I need to know if I'm leaving a child in a potentially unsafe environment, or decide if someone is trying to deceive me into thinking it's safer than it is. And I know this is different, but I'm used to listening to my gut, too, Calloway. And it's telling me that even if you're not sharing everything... I should trust you, too."

For a brief second, a mix of emotions waged a war in the Mountain Man's stormy eyes. Relief. Worry. Fierce want. Frustration.

Then he kissed her forehead and strode across the cabin.

Keira considered going after him, but something told her she didn't have to. Calloway wasn't holding his secrets as tightly as he had been, just hours earlier, and she could be patient.

She leaned her head down on the pillow and

squished up against the wall, making room for him. Whenever he was ready.

GRAHAM BUSIED HIMSELF with tasks around the little house. None of them really needed doing, but none of them took him very far from Keira, either.

He wasn't so bogged down in denial that he didn't recognize the burgeoning feelings he had for the injured girl. Nor was he naive enough to believe that a relationship between them was possible.

Which was a good enough reason for not climbing in beside Keira.

The bigger problem was: it wasn't a good enough reason to stop him from *wanting* to do it. From wanting *her*.

He paused in his counting of his emergency candles to look over at her. She was pushed to the far end of the single-size bed, leaving just enough room for Graham's body. More than enough room if he wrapped his arms around her and held her close.

Her position on the bed wasn't an accident. It was an invitation. One that made an uncomfortable ache spread out from his chest and threaten to take over the rest of him.

You owe her an explanation.

Yes, she deserved some honesty about who he was and what he was doing there.

He just wasn't sure how he was going to go about telling her.

He leaned forward and put his head in his hands.

There just didn't seem to be an easy way of letting someone know you'd been accused of murder.

His eyes slid over Keira, then away from her.

And abruptly, he went still.

Maybe he wouldn't have to tell her after all. Maybe she knew already.

A box—one he'd shoved aside and forgotten about and hadn't touched in long enough to let it get covered in dust—sat across the room, its lid askew.

KEIRA WOKE TO FIND the bed empty and she couldn't quite deny her disappointment that Calloway's warm body wasn't beside her. And her heart dropped even further when she sat up and spied him slumped over a cup of coffee. He was still dressed in the previous evening's clothes, his hair wild.

Did he sleep at all?

"Calloway?"

He turned her way, and she saw that his face was as ragged as his appearance.

"I need to ask you something, Keira."

"Carte blanche?" she replied, managing to keep her voice on the lighter side.

He nodded, but instead of asking a question, he made a statement. "Holly Henderson."

The murdered woman from Derby Reach. Keira felt the blood drain from her cheeks. Why was he bringing her up now?

"You know the name." Calloway said that like a statement, too, but Keira seized on it.

"Yes. I know her name. But so does every person in a hundred-mile radius of Derby Reach.

And you saw my driver's license, so you know that's where I'm from."

"True enough. Holly Henderson was killed four years ago," Calloway said. "Big news in Derby Reach. And you're right, everyone did hear about it. But for some reason, I think it's a little fresher in your mind. When was the last time you heard the name, Keira?"

Without meaning to, she flicked her eyes toward the corner of the room. Toward the box full of incriminating news articles. Immediately, she regretted the slip. Calloway's gaze followed hers. And when he looked back in her direction, his face was dark.

Not with guilt, Keira noted. Regret, yes. Sorrow, absolutely. And hurt. Yes, there was that, too.

And it managed to cut through her apprehension and froze her tongue to the roof of her mouth. Before she could regain the ability to speak, Calloway was on his feet, moving toward her. He reached down, grabbed the rope she'd all but forgotten about and looped it around her wrists. He cinched it just shy of too-tight and fastened her there. Lastly, he snapped up the box, gave Keira a furious, achingly heartbreaking glare and stormed out of the cabin.

Damn, damn, damn.

For several long minutes, she stared at the door. Her heart was still beating at double time, and she was sure he was going to come running back any second and offer an explanation.

What *was* his connection to Holly? For some reason, she was sure—so sure—that he wasn't responsible for her death.

But the door stayed shut, and the cabin stayed distinctly quiet, and she had to resign herself to the fact that he wasn't returning anytime soon. And she wanted to get free.

Keira followed the length of rope with her eyes.

It disappeared at the edge of the bed, so she shimmied toward the end. She still couldn't see where it was tied, but sliding to the edge of the mattress gave her enough slack to move a little more. She inched forward so that her whole head hung off the bed.

Aha!

There it was. The rope went from her wrists to the woven metal frame underneath the mattress. As Keira leaned down a little farther in search of a possible way to free herself, she lost her balance and toppled to the wood floor.

She decided to take advantage of her new position.

She worked her way under the bed, ignoring both the few slivers that found their way into her back and the fact that the frame was low enough to the ground that it dug into her chest.

She brought her fingers to the knot on the bed frame. It was as solid as the one on her hands. But a warped piece on the metal bed frame caught Keira's eye.

If she could twist it, even just a little bit, she might be able to create a gap wide enough to slip the rope through.

She began to work the metal. It hurt a bit. The fibers of the robe rubbed unpleasantly against her skin, and she jabbed herself twice on the metal, hard enough the second time to draw blood.

C'mon, c'mon.

When she finally saw some progress—a tiny space between the bits of metal—tears of relief pricked at her eyes.

With an unladylike grunt, she twisted the already bent piece of metal frame as hard as she could while shoving the rope forward at the same time. It sprung free.

"Yes!" she crowed, and propelled herself out from under the bed.

She crossed the room quickly, but paused at the spot that had housed the cardboard box.

Knowing it probably wasn't the best idea, but unable to resist an urge to do it anyway, Keira made her way to the front door. She cracked it open and a blast of chilly air slammed into her.

Too cold.

She snapped up the Gore-Tex jacket from its hook just inside, put Calloway's too-big boots back on and stepped onto the patio.

She limped down the stairs and into the yard, holding her arms tightly against her chest to fend off the cold.

How Calloway was able to stand it with no coat was beyond her.

Where had the man gone to anyway?

There were plenty of footprints at the base of the stairs and along the edge of the cabin, but no distinct ones that led away from the cabin.

She scanned the tree line. It was so thick that, had it not been for the tracks in the snow, Keira wouldn't have been able to tell where Dave, Calloway's not-so-friendly friend, had come in on his snowmobile. There was no evidence of a footpath in, either. But there had to be a way out. Didn't there?

She had the uneasy suspicion that if she climbed up one of the very tall trees surrounding her and looked out, she would see nothing but even more trees for miles on end.

Keira shivered, a renewed niggling of doubt brought in by the yawning forest before her. Her stomach churned nervously, too, and she had to look away from the suddenly oppressive view of the woods.

Trying to distract herself, she turned back to the cabin and planted her feet in the snow at the bottom of the stairs so she could give the wooden structure a thorough once-over. It *was* old. She'd noted it in the dark the night before. The logs were all worn smooth, and the roof sagged in some places.

But it wasn't falling down at all.

In fact, it looked like someone had made an effort to keep it looking rough while in fact re-inforcing it. Near the top of a particularly high snowdrift, several strips of fresh wood had been nailed over top of one area, presumably to fix a hole. Even though the porch was covered in leaves and debris, it was actually quite new, with no sign of rot. The window from which Keira had watched Calloway argue with the armed man had a new frame, too. The front door was marked with pitting and the hinges looked rusty. But Keira knew that it was solid on the inside. The whole interior was airtight.

To the casual observer, the cabin appeared run-down. Not worth a second glance. But examining it closely, knowing what was on the inside...

"He's not just hiding something," Keira murmured. "He's hiding *himself.*"

She took one more step back. And bumped right into Calloway.

Chapter Thirteen

When Keira stumbled, Graham's hand came up automatically to steady her, then stayed on her elbow.

"For almost four years," he said, his voice full of poorly disguised emotion.

She twisted a little in his grip, but not to get away. Just to face him.

"Since just around when Holly Henderson and her son were killed," Keira stated softly.

He met her gaze. What *had* she seen inside that box? What had she read and then believed? And why the hell did what she thought matter so much more to him than the fact that she'd had a peek into his darkest secrets?

"Calloway?" she prodded.

Graham's heart burned a little inside his chest as he replied. "Yes. You're right. Since they were killed."

"She was your wife, wasn't she?" Keira asked gently.

Graham closed his eyes. "Yes."

"I'm sorry."

"Me, too."

There was a brief pause, and Graham wondered if his agreement had seemed like a confession. An apology. It wouldn't be the first time. But her next words, spoken in a devastated voice, refuted the idea.

"And the little boy…"

"Not my biological son." He opened his eyes again and saw that the pain on her face was genuine. "But I loved him like one. Every day for the last four years, I've ask myself if I could've done something differently. Something to save him."

"Four years…" Keira said. "And you've been on the run ever since."

"Not on the run," Graham corrected bitterly. "Running implies forward movement. I've been hiding, just like you said."

More than hiding.

Graham was stagnant. Stuck in the woods, surrounded by nothing but his own haunted thoughts.

When had he gone from using the cabin as a headquarters to using it as a home? He'd never meant for it to be permanent. Just a place to stay while he hung back as the details sorted themselves out. As Dave Stark did the legwork and searched for the man responsible for Holly's and Sam's deaths.

Graham had wanted to feel useful. He'd started collecting the newspaper articles, brought in by Dave, and made the scrapbook to keep things linear. He was so sure something in those stories would spark something in *him*, and set off a chain of events that would lead to proving he had nothing to gain from his wife's death.

A motive.

That's what he'd been looking for, hidden under the piles of half-truths.

Instead, the perpetual hounding, the mudslinging, all of the ignorant hatred directed Graham's way, laid out in black and white—and sometimes color, too—left him with the feeling that he would never become a free man. Not truly. How could he, with the details of every mistake he'd ever made on display for the whole world to see?

The collection of articles had the opposite effect that it should have anyway. The finger pointers seemed right instead of wrong. Graham understood why they hounded him, why the accusations came hurling his way. His and Holly's unhappiness was well documented. Hell, sometimes it was on public display. Some of it was on paper. If Graham had been on their end, he would be giving himself the exact same scrutiny.

Insurmountable.

That word was tossed around a lot and it stood out to Graham particularly. It's what the evidence had become. It's what his circumstances had become. The reason he felt it was better to stay here, locked behind his cabin door, rather than face a jury and tell a story that seemed unlikely, even to him.

When Graham realized just how desperate—how insurmountable—his situation had become, he'd tossed everything into that damned box and pushed it into a corner.

Before long, the media attention died off, and with the waning interest in the murder, the clippings became few and far between. There was a little resurgence on the anniversary date each year, but aside from that, Graham had nothing to add to his collection.

Ignoring the box had become easy.

Except he couldn't ignore it anymore. Keira had opened it. Now she was staring at him, worry and curiosity plain on her face.

"Just ask me," Graham commanded gruffly.

"Ask you what?"

"The same question that every person who ever heard the story, who ever saw the news, who ever read an article in that box has asked me."

Graham braced himself for her version of it.

Did you kill them? Were you angry? In a fight? Was it an accident, maybe?

Instead, she looked him square in the face and said, "I don't think it's my turn, actually."

Graham couldn't keep the surprise from his reply. "Your turn?"

Was she kidding? Deliberately misleading him?

"I wasn't really counting anymore," she told him, her voice serious. "But I think I owe you at least one."

He thought for just a minute. She wasn't the only one who could throw a curveball.

"Are you still a six out of ten?"

"Is that what you really want to know?"

"Right this second...yes."

Keira pursed her lips as if she was really considering it. "Still a six."

Graham frowned. "I don't know if it's better than a six or worse than a six, but I know you're lying again."

"You sound awfully sure of that."

"I *am* awfully sure of it," he countered and took a step closer to her so he could run a thumb over her cheekbone. "When you lie, you get a little spot of red right *here*."

"I do *not*."

"You do."

The color bloomed further, covering the rest of her cheeks. He didn't release her face, and she didn't pull away. Graham stroked the curve of crimson. His palm cupped her cheek, the tips of his long fingers reaching just above her delicate brow and his wrist at her chin.

A perfect fit.

"Ask me something *real*, Calloway," she said. "Something you really want to know."

"Did you know I was up here, when you came?" Graham replied. "Did someone tell you where to find me?"

Keira's eyes widened. "No! Why would I... No."

The blush drained from her face, and Graham knew she was telling the truth. He released her face with a sigh. The realization disappointed him—no, not disappointed. That wasn't the right description. It sent a swarm of angry wasps beating through his chest, and he couldn't pinpoint the reason.

"Let me show you something," he said.

Graham didn't give her a chance to respond. He slid his hand down her shoulder, then her arm, then threaded his fingers through hers. He guided her gently to the back of the house, following an unnamed compulsion.

The box of newspaper clippings sat just where he'd tossed it, right between his wood bin and the rear of the cabin. Graham ignored it.

"Right there," he stated.

He let go of Keira's hand and pointed at a snow-free, almost perfectly circular patch in the snow at the bottom of the cabin. It wasn't huge and only seemed out of place when looking directly at it. Anyone walking by wouldn't even notice the anomaly.

Graham watched as Keira's stare traveled upward and landed on a narrow spigot, sticking out from between two of the log beams. A nearly indiscernible puff of steam floated from the metal cylinder, then dissipated into nothing.

"You could put your hand right into that and it wouldn't even burn," Graham told her.

"What is it?"

"It's what you don't see up on the roof," Graham replied.

Her eyes widened with immediate understanding. "That little bit of steam comes from that big fire in the stove?"

"That. Or from out here."

Graham bent down and lifted up a large, flat stone, revealing a hidden, in-ground fire pit.

"Oh!" Keira exclaimed.

Still not 100 percent certain why he was doing any of it, Graham snapped up the cardboard box and moved it a little closer to the pit.

It was high time he got rid of them. They'd never done him any good anyway. Only served as a reminder of how very little had been done in solving the case.

He slipped the lid off and reached inside for a stack of newspaper. Then he tossed it into the pit.

"I modified the woodstove into a rocket stove with a heating component. So I feed the fire— from inside or from outside—and the fire exhausts into a specialized section of wall, where it then helps to heat the house. It cools significantly before it's finally filtered out, and by the time it gets *here*, it's not much more than vapor," he explained as he grabbed some more paper. "It took a year to do it, and it was worth the time."

Graham reached into the box once more, and as he did, his hand hit something cool and metal. He shoved his hand into the mess a little farther and yanked out a familiar container.

The flask was silver. Real silver, trimmed with real gold.

A little shake told Graham it was still full.

He disregarded the nagging voice in his head that pointed out that it was barely even noon, twisted off the cap and downed a healthy gulp of the amber liquid inside.

The Macallan.

It was a Scotch Graham would never choose for himself. Just like the flask, the drink inside was a gift from his wealthy father-in-law, a man who had never tired of putting Graham into his lower place on the evolutionary scale. A man who perpetuated the witch hunt that drove him underground.

Even the smooth flavor couldn't quite drive away the bitterness that came with it. Which was the very reason he'd dumped it into the box in the first place. To stash away the memories.

He took another swig, then offered it to Keira.

"If that's what you gave me the night before last," she said, "count me out. I don't want to wind up drunk and tied to another bed."

Graham managed to smile through his beard. "I'm afraid I only have the one bed. My alternatives are a wooden chair and a closet full of flannel."

He meant it as a joke, but Keira shot him a serious, searching look. "Or not tying me up at all."

"That would require a certain level of trust."

She didn't avert her gaze. "Does it look like I'm going anywhere?"

And Graham suddenly realized what he was showing her. What he was telling her. Why it made him wish she hadn't found him by accident.

Because it means I really am the one putting her in danger.

"Does it look like I'm offering to let you leave?"

Her eyes went a little wider as she caught the underlying darkness in his voice. He held out the flask again.

"This is plain old whiskey. Liquid courage." He sloshed it around.

"Do I need to be courageous?" Her question made her sound anything but.

"Always," Graham told her firmly.

Keira took the whiskey. Graham waited until she took a sip before he spoke again.

"My great-grandfather built the cabin here for its inaccessibility. He told no one but his son—who told my dad, who told me—it was here. And as close as the resort is, to get to this spot, you need an ATV in the summer or a snowmobile in the winter. Or you need to *crash* in, I guess, like you did. And who wants to make that kind of effort? So no one knows it's here. No one knows *I'm* here."

"No one except for the man with the gun," Keira pointed out.

He met her eyes. "Him. And now you. Which is a bad combination, I think."

"A bad combination?" Keira parroted.

Graham nodded. "They found what was left of your car."

Fear crossed her face, and he knew she was thinking about the consequences of being found. But she covered it quickly. "Who did?"

"The police found it. The man with the gun— Dave Stark—told me."

"The police? They'll come looking for me and—" She stopped abruptly, relief replaced by worry. "That's not good for you, is it?"

"No, it's not."

"Which is what makes it bad for me, too."

Graham nodded slowly. "I can't let them find me up here. And I can't let Dave get to you, either. As much as I rely on him, I'm not sure he'd make the right decision."

That same bit of fleeting fright passed through her features. "Who is he?"

"A friend. And a business associate, I guess. I pay him well to do the things he does for me. Food. Supplies. Information. Someone I trust." Graham paused, wondering if the last was still true. He heaved a sigh, then went on. "He suspects you're here, Keira. If he finds out he's right, I think it will upset the balance between us."

"Just tell him he's wrong."

"It's not that simple. Dave came up here because he was expecting *me* to come to him."

"Why?"

"He found the man we've been looking for— the one who actually killed Holly and Sam. He's come back to Derby Reach." Graham shook his head. "I'm going after him."

Keira stared back at him and swallowed nervously. Damn, how he hated being the source of her fear.

"What are you going to do to him?" she asked.

Graham had a list of what he'd *like* to do, and none of it was pleasant. But he wasn't that man.

"I'm going to get a confession," he said. "I'm going to find irrevocable proof. And I'm going to let Dave take him in."

"That's where you were going when you found me," Keira stated.

"Yes."

"I'm sorry."

"No. I'm sorry, Keira," he said softly.

She took a small step away. "You are? Why? This means what? That you're holding me hostage?"

"Not because I want to."

"You could just let me go," Keira suggested.

"And then what?"

"And then I walk away."

"Keira, just the accident by itself left too much of a chance that the wrong someone will poke their nose around and find my place. Which is what Dave pointed out. And I can't keep you *here*, either."

"I won't tell anyone about the cabin. You could always take me back to the crash site and I'll find my way out from there."

"And you'll do this wearing what? *My* clothes? Or that tiny dress you had on that's barely more than a rag now? And how will you explain these stitches on your leg?"

He knew his words had an edge again, and he tried to soften them by reaching for her. But she jerked away, and that cut to the quick.

"I could tell them I don't remember," she offered, the worry in her tone growing stronger.

"Selective amnesia?"

"Yes."

"Even if that wasn't as ridiculous as it sounds… could you make it believable?" Graham asked. "Could you make them think you'd forgotten me? I sure as hell couldn't forget you, Keira." He didn't give her time to respond to the admission. "Besides that…even if they bought the story, it would spike their curiosity, don't you think? A young woman miraculously survives when her car goes over a cliff. She not only lives, but receives medical attention. You think the cops will just walk away from that?"

"But if you don't let me go…they'll think I'm dead," she whispered.

"I'm aware of that possibility."

"So why *did* you even bother to save me, Calloway, if you're just going to hold me prisoner forever?"

Graham heard the desperation in her voice and when he answered, he heard it in his own, too. "Redemption."

The word hung between them, meaning so much, but saying so little.

Chapter Fourteen

In spite of what she'd said just minutes earlier, Keira found her feet moving away from Graham. She wasn't running. Not really. She just needed to clear her head. But she still ignored him as he called after her.

She knew with absolute certainty that Graham hadn't killed his wife and son. She'd felt no need to ask when prompted.

But she also had a job and a life. Kids in the system who counted on her. And she sure as heck didn't want her family to assume she was dead. Just the thought of her mom hearing about the accident made her heart squeeze.

But she also knew she wouldn't expose his secret location. She couldn't risk his life just to go back to her own. Not if she could avoid it.

Not that Calloway was about to let her go anyway.

And suddenly she *was* running again. Not away, but as a release of emotion. Back around the house and toward the woods.

It only took seconds for Calloway to catch up to her. His arms closed around her waist, and he spun her to face him. She railed against his hold, her small fists driving into his wide chest. He let her do it. His hands ran over her head and through her hair, and he whispered soothing things as she let all the emotion, all the stress of the past few days fly from her body into his.

At last her energy waned, and she stopped fighting him off. It wasn't what she wanted to be doing anyway. She realized that at the same second she realized she was crying. Soft sobs that shook her shoulders.

She inhaled deeply, trying to stop the tears, and Calloway adjusted, sliding his hands to the small of her back. As if she belonged in his arms.

As if they belonged together. As she looked up at him, his expression was soft.

"Have you noticed that every time you try to hurt me, you wind up in my arms?" Calloway asked, somehow teasing and serious at the same time.

"Have *you* ever noticed that I keep trying to get away?" Keira breathed, and now she could *feel* the telltale spots of color in her cheeks that went along with the lie.

"You sure about that?"

Keira shook her head, not sure if she was answering his question, or if she was just expressing her frustration with the whole situation.

"I've been meaning to ask you…were you really going to club me to death with that fire iron yesterday?" Calloway asked.

Keira managed a smile. "I was going to aim for your legs. I just wanted to knock you down."

"A peg?" This time, there was no mistaking the teasing tone.

"That, too," Keira confirmed.

He touched her face, cupping her cheek with a familiarity that warmed her insides.

"I just want to keep you safe," he said.

His sincerity almost made her break down again.

"Two days ago," she said, sounding as choked up as she felt, "I woke up thinking I knew where my life was going. *Exactly* where it was going. But today, it's like I woke in someone *else's* life."

"Every day," Calloway murmured, his voice heavy with understanding. "That's the exact feeling I've had every day for four years. It's been a living hell for me. Waking up thinking it will be the one when the truth comes out. Wanting justice. Or, if I'm being honest, craving revenge. I can't even remember if it started that way, or if time somehow changed it. Changed *me*. It's been so long since I even thought about anything else that I'm not sure. Yesterday, I could've had it. Revenge. But I saw you in that car. Pretty and fragile and so still. I pulled you out before I could even think about whether it was the right thing to do, considering my situation. It was instinct, I guess. I wasn't even sure you were still alive until I saw the blood seeping from that wound on your leg. Saving you reminded me that there are other things out there for me. You gave me purpose, Keira."

He said her name like he owned it, and her pulse skittered nervously through her veins.

Had any man ever looked as good as Calloway did right that second, with his brooding eyes and his half-apologetic frown? Had anyone else ever put themselves in danger to save her life? Had she ever been someone's *purpose*?

Even though he wasn't holding her tightly anymore, his eyes still held her pinned in place. And she felt a tether form between them. An inexplicable, inescapable bond from her heart to his.

Keira tilted her head in his direction. His lips were less than an inch from hers. She could feel his warm breath on her cheek. She could see the longing in his eyes. His whole body was tense with need. But he didn't make a move.

Keira was sure it should be her, not him, who was offering the most resistance. After all, it had only been two days since she decided she might date Drew. Might marry him. Though it felt like a lifetime now. And Calloway had been alone for a long time. Four years since his wife died, and who knew how many of those he'd spent in isolation?

But in the end, it was Keira who reached for him.

She threaded her fingers into his thick hair, stifling a little moan at how warm and soft it was, and how the longer bits curled against the back of her hand. She made herself caress it only lightly, afraid he was going to pull away. But he didn't. He leaned into the attention for a moment, pressing the back of his head into her palm. Then he let her explore the contours of his lips in slow motion, her mouth tasting his and igniting something in her that was so hot she was surprised the snow underneath them wasn't melting.

Calloway's hands slid over her shoulders, gently kneading her sore muscles, mindful of her most damaged areas. For the first time, Keira was glad he'd stripped her down without asking. He knew where her bruises and scrapes were, and his fingers were adept at avoiding them. But his hands never stopped moving.

They traversed over Keira's face and smoothed her hair back from her face. They tripped softly over her shoulders and down to her hips, not quite tickling, then slipped between the enormous jacket and the borrowed T-shirt to rest on her hips before sliding out again to creep up to her throat.

It was an incredible feeling, to be touched like that. His palms and the strong pads of his fingers and thumbs laid claim to Keira. They worshipped her. She wanted it to go on forever, and when Calloway finally pulled away, a regretful sigh escaped her lips.

GRAHAM STARED DOWN at Keira, committing her features to his memory. He wanted to keep that worshipful expression—the one that believed in him, that trusted him—in his mind forever.

Kissable lips.

Curved cheeks.

Elegant nose with just the slightest bump, making it interesting.

And her eyes. God, they were stunning.

Green, so vibrant and dark, they looked like the Caribbean Sea after sunset, and in the cold sun, her hair was like a crown of fire.

This time, Graham was perfectly content to let himself have the poetic moment.

In mere days, her fiery temper and moments of vulnerability and misleadingly fragile appearance had gotten under his skin. He could barely wrap his head around how badly he felt the need to protect this girl he still knew so little about. He needed more of her story.

"Tell me what you were running from in that little purple car of yours," he commanded softly. "What was so bad that you were willing to risk your life by going out in that storm?"

She looked away. "Lately the only thing I've been running from is you."

Graham knew she was trying to deflect his question. "Do I need to bring out the list of checks and balances to see whose turn it is to ask a question?"

"No." Her chest rose and fell as she took a breath and went on. "His name is Drew. And I wasn't running *from* him, I was running *to* him."

Graham couldn't keep a hint of jealousy out of his voice. "Boyfriend?"

"Potential."

"Does he appreciate your very recent total and complete disregard for your own life?"

"No."

Jealousy morphed into irritation, which was ridiculous. He couldn't dampen it, though.

"Drew must be a complete idiot," he grumbled.

Keira smiled a small smile. "No. That's not it. He just didn't know I was coming."

Graham touched each upturned corner of her mouth before asking, "So you drove all the way up here, unbeknownst to Drew, based on potential?"

"Kind of."

"Kind of yes, or kind of no?" Graham teased.

"It seems silly now," Keira replied.

"Tell me anyway."

"I thought maybe I was meant to be with him," she admitted. "I thought I saw a sign."

"Fate?"

She blushed. "Something like that. It was dumb, though. I took a chance, and instead of it being a sign, I wound up here."

"You don't think it could *still* be fate?"

The blush worked its way from her cheeks down to her throat. "You think my near-death experience was fate?"

"You know that's not what I meant, Keira. And to tell you the truth…I just straight up don't believe in coincidence, Keira. Fate, though, I'm onboard with, one hundred percent."

The pink of her blush extended from her throat to the top of her chest. Graham had an urge to reach up and unzip the rest of the jacket just to see how far down the pretty color went. He closed his hands into fists to stop himself from doing it.

"So what's fate got lined up for me next, then?" she asked softly.

"Getting you somewhere safe," Graham replied. "Somewhere that the man who killed Holly and Sam wouldn't be able to get anywhere near you."

"I'm sorry, Calloway."

"*You* are?"

She nodded. "If I hadn't been so reckless, taking off in the snowstorm when I did—"

Graham cut her off. "Listen. It was stupid of me to save you, Keira. Risky as hell. But it was *my* risk to take." He paused, released her to run both hands through his hair, then spoke again. "I'm glad I did it. In four years, nothing has seemed as real as the moment you opened your eyes and I realized you were alive."

Keira reached up and put a hand on his face, that same look of awe and appreciation on her, and forget unzipping her coat—it took all of Graham's willpower to stop himself from lifting her up and carrying her straight to his too-lumpy bed.

"In fact," he added gruffly, "you're the realest damned thing I've been around for as long as I can remember. So I don't ever want you to be sorry on my behalf."

She opened her mouth, but Graham didn't get to hear whatever she'd been about to say.

A boom echoed around them, and without taking the time to think, he threw himself into her, knocking her to the ground and shielding her with his much larger body. There was a long moment of silence, and Graham wondered if he was being paranoid. There were minor avalanches in the area all the time.

But as he jumped into a defensive crouch, a second bang—possibly closer than the first—shook the air.

It was a gun, no doubt about it. Not the first time he'd heard one out here, but the first time it had seemed so close.

And it's nowhere near *hunting season.*

Was someone firing *at* them?

It seemed unlikely, but…

A third shot rang through the air, and Graham was certain this one was closer again. Keira moved, then let out a muffled shriek as Calloway slammed into her and knocked her to the ground again.

"Can you do something for me?" he asked in a low voice.

"But—"

"Please."

After a breath, her head bobbed against his chest in assent.

"Stay down until I say otherwise."

He felt her nod again and he eased off her body. He was reluctant to let her go, even a little bit, but he needed to assess where the shots were coming from and figure out if they were targeted.

He scanned what little he could see. It wasn't much. The trees provided a perfect hiding place for a shooter. But Graham could use them, too. He and Keira could move quickly between them, using them for cover. If he could figure out which direction the shots came from, they could duck from tree to tree until they reached the cabin. Then Graham would shield Keira again. He'd grab his rifle and—

The rest of his thought was lost as a fourth shot rang out.

Bloody hell.

Graham yanked Keira to her feet, shoved her to the other side of the wide evergreen, then positioned himself in front of her, shielding her from whatever was about to come next.

Chapter Fifteen

As much as Keira preferred to think of herself as strong, she was indescribably grateful to have Calloway between her and whoever was shooting at them. She was shaking so hard, her teeth were chattering, and Calloway was reassuringly solid.

Solid, yes. But not bulletproof, pointed out a small voice in her head.

Her hand slid up to his back, and she opened her mouth to remind him of that fact. But without looking, his hand closed on her wrist, stopping her midway. As if he could sense her movement before she even followed through.

The air was eerily silent now, and they stood like that for what felt like an eternity.

Is it over? Keira wondered.

Calloway spoke in a hushed voice, his eyes still scanning the forest. "You all right back there?"

Keira took a measured breath. "If it wasn't for someone potentially shooting at me in the middle of a forest... Nine out of ten on the sliding scale."

There was a pause, then, in spite of the situation, Calloway let a wry chuckle. "Are you going to tell me what gets me that all-important tenth point? Or am I going to die not knowing?"

"One small thing," Keira breathed.

"Which is?"

"Just keep us alive."

"Nothing would make me happier."

There was another long silence, then Keira asked, "Do you think someone found you?"

He spoke right beside her ear. "I don't know. If they did... Keira. Did you mean what you said about trusting me?"

She managed a nod.

"Good. Because I need you to do something for me."

"What?"

"Run."

Keira blinked. "What?"

"If someone *is* firing at us, it's me they're after," Calloway stated. "I'm going to go in one direction, into the woods. You're going to count to ten and go in the other, toward the cabin."

"I'm not going to do that!"

"Yes, Keira. You are."

He didn't wait for her to argue anymore. He took off across the snow, leaving Keira counting to ten silently, a little more dread filling her with each number.

GRAHAM LOPED OVER the terrain, waiting for another shot to come his way and cursing his own stupidity. He'd left them exposed. He'd put Keira's life in danger even though he'd been trying to do the opposite.

He didn't bother to hide as he dodged from tree to tree. If the shooter was looking for him, he wanted his undivided attention. And to put some distance between Keira and the bad end of the gun.

"C'mon," he growled. "Follow *me*. Shoot at *me*."

The woods were silent except for the sound of his own feet hitting the ground. He finally slowed, acknowledging that maybe—a big maybe—he'd been overreacting. That possibly some off-season hunter had taken advantage of the aftermath of the snowstorm and was on his side of the mountain in search of some big game.

But what if he wasn't?

What if, somehow, the man who'd taken Holly and Sam from him found him? Found *them*?

Graham moved faster, getting angrier at himself by the second. Which is why he didn't notice the armed man in front of him until they were just a foot apart.

When he did spot him, Graham didn't stop to think. He just reacted, determined to use his strength to overpower the assailant, gun or no gun. It wasn't until he'd already pounced on the other man and smacked the weapon away that he recognized him.

Dave.

"What the *hell* is going on?" Graham demanded.

His friend was sucking wind, and when he opened his mouth, all that came out was a groan.

Graham eased off. "Explain yourself."

"Talk. To. You," Dave wheezed.

"And you were getting my attention by shooting at me?"

"Not. Me."

"Who?"

"Don't. Know."

Graham resisted an urge to shake a proper answer from him friend.

"Heard shots," Dave offered, still inhaling rapidly.

"Did you see the shooter?"

He finally seemed to have caught his breath, shaking his head. "Maybe it was a hunter. But it doesn't matter. You have to admit that it's too risky to stay here now. I can tell from your face that you know it."

Graham exhaled. Keira was safe. At least for the moment.

He opened his mouth to ask what Dave was doing back so soon—what he wanted to talk about—but before Graham could get an explanation, an engine sputtered to life in the distance, and both men turned toward the sound.

KEIRA TIGHTENED HER already strained grip on the handlebars of the snowmobile. The seat was icy under her bare legs, but she ignored the discomfort. She needed to get the vehicle moving, to get it to Calloway. She'd run blindly, obeying this command even though so many parts of her mind—of her heart—protested against it. But halfway back to the cabin, she'd spotted the big machine. It was not quite hidden behind a low bush, and it seemed like a godsend. A way to get both of them to safety. Quickly.

"How hard can it be?" she muttered aloud to herself as she looked over the components another time. "Throttle. Choke. Kill switch if I need it."

She squeezed the gas, just a little, and the machine bucked as the skis snuck to the snow.

"Easy," she cautioned, not sure if she was still speaking to herself or if she was talking to the snowmobile.

She supposed either would work.

Keira climbed off, moved to the front of the vehicle and kicked away some of the snow blocking the way, then climbed back on.

She put a little more pressure on the throttle, and the machine jerked forward hard enough to send her flying against the handlebars. She held on for dear life as it rode forward a few feet, then stalled.

Damn.

Tears threatened to form in her eyes, and Keira forced them back. She didn't have time to waste being upset. Angrily, she pulled out the choke, yanked on the pull starter as hard as she could and willed the stupid thing to cooperate.

It roared to life, and this time when she closed her fingers over the throttle, she did it softly. The snowmobile slid over the snow at a crawl. It growled a little as she held it steady.

Apparently her options were very slow or very fast. No in between.

So, fast it was.

Keira gritted her teeth and squeezed.

GRAHAM WATCHED IN awed horror—and with more than a little bit of admiration, too—as the enormous piece of machinery came tearing around the corner. Keira sat atop it, her stance awkward, her eyes almost closed and her hair flying out behind like a blazing red cape.

Her beautiful determination was clear, even through her obvious fear.

Then she spied him, and her eyes were no longer half-shut. They were so wide that their green hue was visible even from where Graham sat.

She seemed to clue in at the same second that Graham did that she was on a crash course, headed straight for him and Dave.

Sure enough, she tipped the handlebars, trying to angle away from them. Her motions became frantic, her arms flailing. Then the snowmobile bucked, and Keira was suddenly barely hanging on, her legs tossed to the side and her hands gripping the bars. The machine bounced along wildly as if it had a mind of its own.

Almost too late, Graham realized that the snarling vehicle was still aimed in his direction. At the last second, he dove toward Dave and shoved the other man out of the line of fire.

He wasn't swift enough to save himself.

The last thing Graham saw before the snowmobile clipped him, and his head exploded in pain, was the terrified look on Keira's face as she flew up and sailed through the air.

I'm sorry, he thought weakly.

But there was nothing he could do as the world blurred and he collapsed to the ground.

Chapter Sixteen

Keira landed hard against a raised snowbank, taking the brunt of the hit straight in the stomach. All of the air left her lungs in one gust, and abruptly she couldn't breathe. She couldn't inhale or exhale or force the oxygen into her body no matter how badly she wanted.

I'm going to die. Calloway's going to die. And it's going to be my fault.

How cruel was *that* for fate?

For a second, the world stayed dark.

Then it was full of spotted pinpricks of light.

And at last, Keira felt her chest rise and fall, and the white-covered ground evened out in her vision.

She pulled herself across the snow until she reached Calloway's still body.

Please let him be okay, she prayed, her heart banging against her ribs so hard it hurt.

She dropped her head to Calloway's chest. It rose and fell evenly, and when Keira put her fingers to his throat, his pulse was strong.

Thank God.

And then a hand landed on her shoulder and Keira remembered they weren't alone.

She brought her eyes up nervously and, through her tears, stared at the man above her.

He looked rough and dangerous, with a cut in the corner of one lip, and one of his eyes looked almost black. Like the kind of man who would be firing a weapon in the woods.

"Ms. Niles," he said.

He knows your name.

And for a second, he looked vaguely familiar.

No. Impossible. She knew no one who matched his description.

"Ms. Niles," he repeated, this time a little more urgently. "Stay calm."

His words had the opposite effect that they should have, and panic set in.

She had to get away.

Keira's eyes flicked around the clearing in search of safety. Of protection.

The snowmobile.

Too complicated.

The cabin.

Too far.

A glint of silver in the snow.

Yes. The gun.

Keira sprang up and hurled herself past the worse-for-wear man in front of her and dove for the weapon. She caught sight of the expression on his face—first full of surprise, then under-standing—and he moved, too.

But Keira was faster.

Her hands closed on the gun and for a second she was thoroughly triumphant.

Thank God.

Then the blond man was on her, one hand wrapped around her ankle and the other claw-ing to get the weapon away from her.

"Don't do something you'll regret," he said through clenched teeth.

"I won't," she promised, then drew back her free foot and slammed it into his chest.

He flew back and Keira leaped up once more. With a sharp stab of remorse about leaving Calloway where he was, she took off at a limping run.

The thump of feet on snow told her that the man was following her. And gaining ground.

C'mon, c'mon, she urged herself.

She was close enough to the cabin that it was a viable option now.

Come! On!

Pushing through the throbbing pain in her thigh, Keira forced herself to keep going. And at last she reached the wooden patio. But as her hand found the doorknob, her head swiveled and she saw that her pursuer had caught up to her.

She spun, cocked the gun and pointed it at the blond man just as one of his feet met the bottom step.

"You're making a mistake," he told her, looking far less frightened than she thought he should.

"I do know how to fire this thing," Keira warned.

"You might want to rethink actually doing it, Ms. Niles."

"People love a good self-defense story," she retorted.

"Maybe. But the law rarely favors people who fire on those working with the police. Especially when they're shooting while in the home of a known criminal."

The police? A criminal?

Keira eyed the other man disbelievingly. Maybe the last part made sense.

Calloway *was* on the run from the police, after all. But nothing about the man standing in front of her screamed law enforcement. No uniform. No readily proffered ID.

No. He has to be lying.

"You expect me to believe that you're a cop?" she asked. "And Calloway is what, then…the robber?"

"This is hardly a game, Ms. Niles. My name is David Stark and—"

The rest of his statement was lost as Keira finally clued in to who this man was.

Dave Stark.

Calloway's friend. His business associate. Whom he'd known for years. And trusted.

A cop?

"I know who you are," Keira said.

"Then you know Graham and I are friends."

"Calloway told me about your business arrangement."

"But he didn't happen to mention that I work for the Derby Reach PD?"

"If you're a cop, and you knew he was here, why haven't you just arrested him?" Keira countered.

"Because I've been his friend for far longer than I've been a policeman. And because I've been helping him for as many years as he's been on the run."

"Prove it," Keira challenged.

"Fine. I have three things in my pocket," he

said. "My badge, my driver's license and a pay stub to prove the ID is real. I'd like to reach in and get them. Do you mind if I do that?"

"Go for it," Keira conceded.

Slowly—as if *she* was the unpredictable one— he unzipped his jacket, pulled it open to give Keira a view of what he was doing, and stuck his hand into a side pocket. Just as slowly, he dragged out a little leather case and held it up. The front flapped open, revealing a gold badge.

He closed it up again, then traded it for a wallet, which he held out to Keira.

"*You* take the stuff out," she ordered.

He complied, first flipping out the plastic-covered license, then unfolding a piece of paper.

Without letting the gun go, Keira moved just close enough that she could read each of them. And as much as she wanted them to be fake, she was sure they were legitimate. "David Rodney Stark. Employee number 102 of the Derby Reach PD." Even Keira's desperate brain couldn't come up with a reasonable explanation for carrying around a phony pay stub.

Her body sagged.

Dammit.

Calloway had been paying a cop to...do what exactly? Bring him mushroom soup and information? Why was the other man even agreeing to it?

Then a low groan came from behind the man in question, and Keira traded in her concern about the cop for concern about Calloway, who was half standing, half slumping on the snow.

GRAHAM LET DAVE slide an arm across his back and guide him into the cabin.

His attention, though, was on Keira.

Her hair was still wild from the crazy ride on the snowmobile. Even though she held a gun in her hand, she'd sucked her bottom lip between her teeth and looked like she was trying not to cry.

Because of you.

If he'd had the energy and the time, he would've cursed himself out for somehow managing to twist the situation so that instead of him worrying about her, she was worrying about him.

But you don't *have time*, he reminded himself. *And you can't protect her, get the cabin ready in case you don't make it back and keep your own body breathing at the same time.*

Which somehow seemed important now. Guns-out revenge wasn't an option. Not if he wanted a chance at something he hadn't thought about in a long time. A future.

So he spoke, and he wasn't sure if it was because of his recent brush with unconsciousness or if it was because he was saying something he really wished he didn't *have* to say, but his words sounded hollow and far away.

"Dave, you need to take Keira off the mountain. Now."

Keira stiffened and her mouth dropped open as if she was going to argue, but Dave beat her to it.

"The crash is all over the news, Graham. Which is what I came here to talk to you about. They're looking for a body, trying to identify the driver. What do you think they're going to do when they find out she's not so dead, after all?"

"You're not going to let them find out. You're going to take her to your hotel and stay there."

His friend ran a frustrated hand through his hair. "I came here to convince *you* to come with me. To remind you again that everything we've been working for is about to slip through our fingers. Not to transport some girl you just met, keep her hidden for you and *still* not accomplish what we've been trying to accomplish for the last four years."

Graham met his friend's eyes. "I'm asking for two days, Dave."

"This has nothing to do with her. You said it yourself just two days ago."

"What other choice is there?"

"Let the cops find her."

"And if they find out who she's been with? If that info gets back to the wrong person before I catch up to him?"

"Graham, something's gotta give. I'm tired of chasing down bad leads and using resources

I have no right to be using. I'm sick of making excuses to my wife and not seeing my kids and worrying all the time that I'm going to get caught helping you. Four years is a long time to live like this. I thought we were done. Now I feel like we're starting up all over again."

Graham's temper flared. "I *lost* my wife, Dave. I *lost* my kid. And you come up here and expect me to lose someone else because you think things have been too hard on *you*? I won't take the risk that Ferguson might get ahold of Keira, too, and use her as leverage. The only way to ensure her safety is to take her away from here."

"You could turn yourself in instead."

Graham's gut clenched. "Turn myself in?"

"You'd rather have me help you with a kidnapping?"

"Stop!"

The emphatic protest came from Keira, who was shaking her head and fixing Graham with an achingly sweet glare. "Calloway isn't turning himself in to save me. He sure as hell didn't kidnap me. And you guys need to quit talking about me like I'm not here and not capable of making my own decisions."

"I can't let you stay here," Graham told her.

"And you can't make me leave," she replied.

He moved closer and lifted a hand to Keira's cheek. "You *have* to do this. It's the only thing that's going to keep you out of danger. Let Dave take you somewhere safe. I promise you, I won't be far behind. I'll take care of what needs to be taken care of and I'll come for you."

"And if you get killed in the process?" Her voice shook. "Calloway, I—"

Graham leaned down and cut her off with a kiss, not caring if Dave was watching. She brought her hands up and buried them in his hair, and he didn't let her go until her could feel her heart thumping through both layers of their clothes.

He leaned away. "I have a damned good reason to stay alive, Keira."

"Two days?" she asked breathlessly.

Graham exhaled and made a promise he hoped he could keep. "Forty-eight hours, no more."

Get in, get Mike Ferguson and get back to Keira. Then he'd figure out his next move.

Minutes later, he bundled her up—thoroughly if not comfortably—and was leading her to the snowmobile. There he kissed her again, this time tenderly, then helped her straddle the vehicle.

Dave looked unhappy, but Graham didn't care. His eyes were stuck on Keira's slim form, and they stayed there as the snowmobile roared to life and the two of them sped off into the thick woods.

Chapter Seventeen

Keira quickly gave up trying to keep a reasonable amount of physical space between herself and Officer David Stark. Her helmeted face was pressed between his shoulder blades, and her legs squeezed his hips. She rode that way not because she was any more comfortable with him than she had been since the first second she'd laid eyes on him, but because he navigated the mountain with reckless abandon.

Trees whipped by in a blur. Snow kicked up and into Keira's shirt, then melted there. It made the wind hit her that much harder and made it that much more necessary to crush herself into Dave's back.

She was holding on to him out of necessity. And she wasn't happy about it.

The only good thing about it was that it helped to keep her mind from everything else. She deliberately blocked out her thoughts and focused on the scenery instead. It was nothing more than a blur of white, and they rode for so long that Keira was sure they were going to run out of gas.

Parts of her were frozen. Parts of her ached. And *all* of her wished she could go back in time to before her accident so she could just go back to being herself. No gunshots, no makeshift stitches, no crazy ache in her chest over a man she just met.

But her concern for Calloway's well-being overrode her efforts. And try as she might, Keira couldn't shake the fact that the most pressing of her worries was that he might never be able to keep his promise and come to her.

So maybe it wasn't that the accident skewed her view. Maybe she'd known all along that Drew wasn't right for her. Maybe she hadn't really been leading a full life at all. It just took crashing into the Mountain Man's life to reveal it.

Somehow, she was sure she could pick any moment from the past few days and attach more meaning to it than she could to any other part of her life.

So, no. She *wouldn't* erase the accident. Because without it—without Drew and her stupid trip to the chalet to make her move—she wouldn't have almost died and she wouldn't have had the best kisses in the world with the most interesting man she'd ever met.

And yes. She'd take those little glimpses of heart-pounding excitement over another twenty-four years of never realizing what she was missing.

As she came to that conclusion, a final blast of snow flew from underneath the snowmobile, and she and Dave ground to a halt.

The seed of doubt in Keira's mind grew as she leaned away from him and took in her surroundings. The trees were well behind them, and there was nothing but a snow-covered hill in front of them.

Keira swung her legs off the snowmobile uncertainly, and Dave did the same, but with far more self-assurance. Then he tipped his goggles to his head and helped her pull off the borrowed helmet.

"Here's the deal, Ms. Niles," he said, his voice sounding extraloud now that the roar of the engine had cut off. "On the other side of that crest is the side road that leads into Mountain View Village. If we head into town, we might be walking straight into a sea of press. But what *I* want is to avoid them—and everyone else—if at all possible."

Keira stared at him. "You're not taking me to the hotel?"

"I want the same thing you do—to protect Graham. And to do that, I think we should steer clear of the resort town altogether. Get you somewhere safe and sound and far away from here," Dave told her.

"But Graham—"

"Hasn't thought this all the way through. Up here, I can't keep you hidden. Not effectively. Too many people are looking for you. If I take you off the mountain completely, I at least stand a chance of keeping you out of the limelight."

Keira waited for him to add something else about Calloway, something hopeful. But he just handed her the helmet again.

"We all set, then?" he asked.

So Keira nodded. She didn't see that she had much of a choice.

As MUCH AS Graham wanted to toss aside everything and throw on his snowshoes and start moving, he knew better.

Four years of waiting had taught him the value of patience, and as desperate as he was to get to Keira, his experience told him that he needed to be prepared. There was no way for him to avoid going back to the place where it all started. But if he had to do it, he could do it right.

He started with his hair, hacking it to nearly respectable length, revealing far more gray than he'd had when he went underground. Then he moved on to his face, shearing it so that the formerly bristly beard was gone completely. When he was done, the skin underneath it was almost raw with the effort.

He bathed head to toe, and though he kept himself fairly well-groomed anyway, he made an extra effort this time to scrub away every ounce of dirt. There was no sign of grime under his nails, no campfire scent lingering on his skin.

Toss on a white coat, Graham thought humorlessly as he gave himself a final once-over, *and I might be able to go straight back to the office.*

Right then, though, he laid out something far more practical. Snow-proof, waterproof pants. Lined, but not so thick that they would impede movement. On top, he'd wear a matching coat with good breathability and a removable interior. Both items were unused—Graham would have to rip the tags off before putting them on— bought long ago with the assumption that one day, he would have to abandon his home. Un-

derneath those, he'd put on running gear, completely practical and also in new condition.

He had sharp jeans, a still-in-the-plastic T-shirt,
and just in case, a dress shirt and tie, ready to go
into his bag.

The cabin itself had been transformed, too.
Graham boarded up the windows, careful to
use well-worn pieces of wood and nails that had
seen better days. He tore apart the bottom step
in a way that made it appear to be natural rot,
and punched a hole through the front part of the
deck, too. He used a shovel to throw up several
mounds of snow in front of the house, as well,
and another snowstorm or two later, they'd look
completely natural.

When Graham glanced up at the sky, he
thought he probably wouldn't have to wait long
for Mother Nature to help him out with that.

Finally, he stood back to survey the house once
more, looking for any other signs that would
give away its most recent use. He was satisfied
that there were none, and anyone who thought

it was worth getting past the snow and the broken patio would be sorely disappointed when they got inside. Everything that *could* be burned, *had* been burned. From the mattress to the curtains to—regretfully—the food, it had all been incinerated.

Only the most necessary items had been saved, and they fit neatly into Graham's backpack beside his extra clothes.

Be Prepared. Back to the Boy Scout analogy.

FROM THE MOMENT Graham drafted his to-do list, to the second he completed it all, took less than four hours.

The sky was dark, the stars a speckled tableau above his head, and he was ready.

Traveling at night wasn't for everyone.

But to quote Dave, this is me *we're talking about.*

Graham turned away from his home, not even bothering with a second look. He'd once walked away from a thirty-year-long life. This was nothing.

THE GRUELING HIKE brought Graham all the way to the edge of the resort town. He was covered in sweat, aching and no less determined.

He kicked out a shallow hole in the snow, then stripped off his travel gear in favor of his jeans and T-shirt. He stuffed his cash and falsified ID into his jacket pockets, and filled the hole with his discarded items and marked the spot with a distinctly shaped rock as big as his head. Graham was sure he could locate it again, but there was nothing personal left in the pack, so if found, it wouldn't arouse suspicion in the finder.

It wasn't ideal, but it would do. It had to.

From his spot, the lights were too close and bright enough to make his head hurt.

No time for self-pity, he growled silently and stepped back into the trees.

Graham traipsed up the road, mentally recalling the name of the hotel Dave used each month.

I'm not going to go in, he told himself.

He just wanted to make sure they got there before he found a way down to the city.

He paused at a large overblown map at the

top of Main Street. He found the place—Rocky Side Hotel—quickly. As he scanned the location, he realized that even if he skirted the perimeter streets all the way in, he'd still have to pass through a very busy area in order to reach the hotel itself. He cursed the fact that Dave had chosen somewhere so public as his monthly stopping point. Mountain View had plenty of more out-of-the-way places to stay. Romantic bungalows. Three-star hotels. The only place more attention-drawing would've been the chalet itself.

Graham forced himself to keep going.

It was well past any reasonable hour to be out on foot anywhere else, but in Mountain View the second the sun went down, the skiers became partiers and they stayed out until it rose again. As a result, even keeping to the edge of town didn't stop Graham from running into people.

After so many years in isolation, it was overwhelming.

So he was nervous. Far more on edge than he should have been.

Maybe he *would* go in. Maybe he'd just check on Keira, then see if Dave had a reasonable line on a vehicle.

And to breathe.

He knew it was ridiculous to assume that someone would know him, but that didn't make the feeling go away. When he finally had no choice but to head into the busy square in front of Dave's hotel, and a grinning club rat caught and held his eye, he expected to see some flicker of recognition. Some frightened spark that said, *Oh, that's him. That's the man accused of killing his wife.*

When he tried to cross a street a little too soon and a stranger grabbed his shoulder to stop him from falling in front of a party bus, he just about punched the Good Samaritan in the face. Even after Graham stumbled through an apology, the wary look didn't disappear from the man's eyes.

Graham didn't breathe easily until he reached the building with the large hand-painted sign that declared it as the correct hotel. His hand closed on the metal door and he pulled. It didn't budge, and when Graham took a step back he saw why.

The Rocky Side Hotel was closed for renovations.

What the hell?

Graham squinted at the sign giving the closure dates. Dave hadn't been there at all. Not in the past thirty days anyway.

So where had he taken Keira? Another hotel?

No.

A sinking feeling hit Graham straight in the gut.

He must have taken her home.

What for? To give her up, like he'd wanted to? For a misguided sense of right and wrong?

Graham reached up to yank on his hair, but came away empty-handed. It was too short for the habit to be satisfying.

His friend *knew* how much danger Keira would be in if Ferguson learned about her. To bring her that much closer, even if he thought it was because he was doing the right thing...

Graham shook his head and took another few

steps away from the closed hotel and smacked into an unsuspecting passerby. The guy stammered an apology, but Graham cut him off by grabbing his arm.

"What's the easiest way to get out of town?" he demanded harshly.

The stranger's eyes widened. "Now?"

"Yes, now."

"It's two in the morning."

"I'm aware."

The man scratched his head, looking drunkenly puzzled, then grinned brightly. "Truck stop!"

"Truck stop?"

"Yeah. The delivery guys come and go all night so they don't mess with the tourist mojo during the day. Six blocks of back alley will get you there."

Graham released his arm. "Thanks."

"No problem."

The partier stumbled away, and Graham moved quickly.

Chapter Eighteen

Keira stared out the window of Dave's car, blurry-eyed. The hours it took to drive from the mountain to Derby Reach had passed quickly, mostly because she'd spent them sleeping. Or *pretending* to be asleep so she wouldn't have to make small talk with the man in the driver's seat.

Now they'd stopped.

But they weren't anywhere near her apartment. It only took Keira a single second of peering into the dim predawn to clue in that they *were* somewhere familiar, though.

"This is my parents' house," she said, sounding as puzzled as she felt.

"I know," Dave replied.

"Why are we here? How did you even know where it was?"

"I looked up a few details about you. One of the perks of being a cop. And as much as I hate the idea, Ms. Niles, I need to leave you alone for a bit to take care of a few details. I figured it was safer to bring you here than it was to drop you at your own place. I hope you don't mind."

Keira's head buzzed with worry. And actually, she *did* mind. It felt like an intrusion of privacy. But she could hardly complain about the policeman doing his job. Assuming that's what he *was* doing. And when had he had time to look up the details of her life? He'd barely left her alone for longer than a bathroom break.

"My own apartment would've been fine," she said a little stiffly.

But Dave shook his head. "And take the chance that some well-meaning neighbor spots you and sees the news and reports it?"

"Right," Keira replied uncertainly.

"Besides. Your parents' house is empty, and this neighborhood is known for its privacy."

A sliver of worry crept up Keira's spine. Had she mentioned her parents' monthlong vacation? Or was that another detail he'd uncovered in his miniature investigation into her life?

And if he can find out those things in a few hours, how come he couldn't prove Calloway's innocence in four full years?

Dave put his hand on her arm, and she flinched.

"If you're worried about Graham finding you...don't. He's as resourceful as he is single-minded. And if things go wrong, having you here instead of at home will give me the extra time I need to get you out safely."

The sliver became a spike. "Wrong?"

"I'm not trying to scare you, Ms. Niles. I want you to feel safe and secure. But I'd be lying if I didn't admit that in the past, Graham has lashed out on the people he thought wronged him. There was a time when I would've called him dangerous. It's been years since he's done anything truly violent, but it's also been years since he had any reason to. He won't give up until either he's taken care of the threat, or until taking care of the threat becomes more dangerous than the threat itself. I don't want you in the middle of that."

Keira opened her mouth, then closed it again. She wasn't sure she agreed with Dave's analysis. Calloway might very well be single-minded, but it was only out of necessity. Who wouldn't want to prove their innocence in a case like this one? And as far as self-preservation was concerned…she was living proof that he was capable of caring more about others' safety than he did about his own.

She had a funny feeling that in spite of what Dave claimed to the contrary, he *was* trying to scare her. She just wasn't sure why.

"Can I trust you, Ms. Niles?" the policeman asked abruptly.

"Trust me?" she replied.

"To lie low until I've done what needs to be done to ensure that there's no danger to you. Or to the people close to you."

His words had an ominous undertone to them, and Keira bit back an urge to point out that leaving her alone seemed counterproductive to keeping her safe. And to be honest, she was just plain eager to be rid of the man.

"I can do that," she agreed.

Dave seemed satisfied. He opened the glove box and pulled out a business card, which he handed to her.

"This is my direct number," he said. "If you have any problems at all, call me first. Do *not* contact anyone else. Do *not* reach out. And most importantly, do *not* tell anyone where you are."

He squeezed her hand. She let him hold it just long enough to not seem unappreciative.

"Thank you," she murmured.

"Another thing," Dave said. "If you doubt what I've said, keep this in mind. Your car might've crashed, but the fire that consumed it was man-made. The cops have ruled it arson. And we both know there was only one man up there."

Keira almost laughed. But then she caught

sight of the serious look on Dave's face. Yes, he was still definitely trying to scare her.

Except for the first time, she was also sure he was telling the truth.

"Like I said, just keep in mind that he's the type of man who will cover up evidence at someone else's expense."

She gave him a level stare. "I'll do that."

Then she pulled away, and as she did, Dave reached for his own seat belt. Keira realized he was probably planning on accompanying her up the driveway. It was the last thing she wanted.

"It's all right," she said quickly. "I'm fine by myself."

"I'd feel better if you let me walk you to the door."

She shook her head and forced what she hoped looked like a genuine smile. "I'm lying low, remember? The last thing we want is my parents' neighbors talking because a strange man is dropping me off. If you come up, they'll have a fit."

Dave frowned, but Keira swung open the door

before he could argue. Then she slammed it shut and ran up the driveway. Without looking back, she retrieved the key hidden under her mom's near-dead potted plant and let herself into the house. She counted to sixty, peeked out the curtains and finally let out a breath when she saw that Dave's car was completely out of sight.

GRAHAM JERKED HIS head up from the condensation-laden window, his hands closing tensely on the jacket between his thighs. He wasn't sure how long he'd been in the restless, close-to-sleep state, but the city lights were visible on the horizon.

"You all right?"

The question—asked in a voice that sounded full of genuine concern—came from the senior-aged trucker who'd agreed to bring Graham down the mountain.

Graham cleared his throat and did his best to answer like a normal person would.

"Fine. Just tired."

"Might wanna ease up on the death grip of the coat, then," said the trucker.

"Thanks for the tip." Graham's reply was dry, but he did let go and force his hands to his knees instead.

The driver was silent for a long moment, staring out the windshield.

Maybe you really are *incapable of normal*, Graham thought.

Seconds later, the trucker confirmed his suspicions. "I don't know what you're running from—or to—and I don't want to. But if you act that suspicious everywhere you go, you can bet the cops'll be on you before you can demand to have your rights read."

"Trust me. I'm so far past the reading-the-right part of things that it's not even funny."

The trucker laughed anyway. "Makes me glad that this is the end of the line, my friend."

He nodded out the front window. A brightly lit truck stop beckoned just a mile or so ahead.

Graham knew the spot. It was just outside Derby Reach.

For the first time since his flight from the cabin, he hesitated. It was there that his original escape started. Five hundred and fifty dollars slipped to another trucker—one far less friendly than the one who sat beside him now—to take him 482 miles.

He'd worked hard to put the town behind him.

Graham had been smart about his movements. Careful. He'd created a trail. Money here and there. Verifiable appearances at gas stations and hotels and grocery stores. One overblown fight in a bowling alley and a faked slipup of credit card use in a city on the other side of the country. Until he deliberately tapered off in his endeavors to be seen. It only took four months to create the perfect wild-goose chase. Two months after that, he was well settled at the cabin. Dave knew where he was, but no one else was looking in the right place. No one was even *thinking* about the right place.

Now I know how they felt, he thought grimly. *Clueless.*

Where would the other man have taken Keira? *Not to her home. Too obviously risky.*

Even Dave would know that.

Graham stared down at his hands, considering all the options.

But not to his own home, either. Keira would never agree to that.

Dave would want her to feel safe. Comfortable. Familiar.

Family.

Had Keira mentioned any? Graham couldn't remember, but his gut told him Dave would've found out. Then what?

"Too many damned possibilities," Graham muttered.

"Buddy?"

Graham's gaze flicked back to the trucker. "Sorry."

"Don't apologize for being scared. We all got stuff to worry us."

Scared?

Graham opened his mouth to deny it, but when he met the trucker's eyes, and the other man gave him a knowing nod, he realized it was true. He *was* scared. For himself, a little. For Keira, a lot.

He held in a growl.

Twenty years, he'd known Dave. Twenty damned years. More than two-thirds of his life. He knew—more than most—that Dave's priorities could get a little skewed at times, but Graham would never have thought he'd do something like this.

Whatever this *is.*

It didn't really matter anyway. Graham was responsible for what had happened to Keira. What might happen to her still. Damn, how he hated this helpless feeling.

I have to save her.

But first he had to find her.

"You sure you're all right?" the trucker asked.

Graham managed a forced smile. "Six out of ten."

The big rig came to a rumbling halt then, and the diner loomed in front of them, and Graham couldn't decide if it felt like a starting point, or the end. He just knew he *needed* it to be the former. Would force it that way if he had to.

"Have they got public internet in there?" Graham asked.

The trucker shrugged, reached into his pocket and handed over a smartphone.

"Not in there. But I've got it out here," he said. "Probably less traceable anyway. You can feel free to clear the browser history after, too."

Graham punched a button on the screen, then paused. One of the last things he wanted was to make this man culpable for his mistakes. The phone became a lead weight in Graham's hand.

"If I told you that you were aiding a fugitive, would you still hand this over?" he asked.

The driver met his eyes evenly. "Been working the routes for forty-two years. Picked up a lot of hitchhikers. Means I'm pretty damned good at two things—navigating the roads and navigating people. If you're one of the bad guys, I'll hand over my license right this second."

"Thanks," Graham replied gruffly.

He fumbled with the phone for a second, but in a couple of taps, he had a home address for H. Gerald and Karen Niles.

And it gave him another chill. Their house was just a block from the home where he'd lived with Holly and Sam.

He shoved aside the increasing concern and, as suggested, he swiped away the browser history before handing the phone back. If nothing else, it gave the man plausible deniability.

The trucker gave him one more long stare. "You sure you don't want to walk away from whatever this is? As soon as I'm done my pie, I'm turning left and going straight for a hundred more miles."

An image of Keira—worried eyes, fiery eyes, soft, caring eyes—flashed through Graham's mind, and any doubt fled once again.

"Thanks," he said. "But some things are more than worth the risk."

The trucker smiled smugly, as if he was expecting the answer and knew just what Graham was talking about. "She must be one hell of a girl."

"Damn right," Graham agreed and hopped from the truck.

A hell of a girl in a hell of a situation. And only another five miles away.

Chapter Nineteen

Keira paced the length of her parents' living room, wishing she could shake the restless feeling that kept her moving.

Everything she normally found comforting about the house was putting her on edge.

The food she'd taken from the freezer, heated according to the note taped to the lid, then eaten, sat heavily in her stomach. It was shepherd's pie. One of her favorites and it had never given her such bad heartburn.

She'd bathed. But the light lavender-scented body wash she'd used reminded her of her mother and made Keira lonely for her. Why had she promised Dave Stark that she wouldn't call anyone? Just hearing her mom's voice, listening to her complain about the heat or the way the humidity made her hair puff out, would've helped. Even if she didn't tell her mom anything, even if she just sat quietly while her mom spoke... it would've gone a long way to ease her mind. But she didn't want to endanger her parents. She didn't even want to risk it.

And now that she was clean and fed, Keira didn't know what to do with herself.

The quiet—so different from the perpetual noise of her thin-walled, one-bedroom apartment—was stifling. And each time an unexpected sound cut into the silence, whether it was the rumble of the furnace or the bark of a neighbor's job, Keira jumped.

Even the twelve snow globes—one for each Christmas they'd spent in Disneyland when she was a kid—that lined the fireplace mantel offered little comfort.

And the policeman's actions and decision had done nothing to ease her worry. He'd created even more questions for her than she'd had before.

Keira sighed, overwhelmed by frustration. For a second, she considered whether or not she should go against her word and sneak over to her apartment. Even if it was just to grab some of her own clothes.

She plucked at the pajamas borrowed from her mom's drawer, wondering if they were part of what kept her from feeling comfortable. From feeling like herself.

She picked up the first snow globe from the mantel and shook the little white flakes over Mickey's head. It was a mistake. The snowy display sent her mind immediately to Calloway.

Was he okay?

Keira set the snow globe down, and her gaze found her parents' antiquated computer in the corner of the living room.

Dave had asked her not to contact anyone. But he hadn't asked her not to research anything on her own.

A little guiltily, she slid out her dad's office chair from its dusty spot under the mahogany desk, sat her still-aching rear end in the cool leather and booted up the old machine. It took several minutes for the thing to chug to life— just enough time to chew one pink nail to a ridiculously short length and to assess whether or not she was being a little crazy.

A police officer had just all but warned her outright how dangerous Calloway was. And really, just the fact that Calloway had a hideout should've been enough to set off a hundred warning bells. Or at least make her question her attraction to him. Instead, every self-preserving instinct she had reared its head when she thought of David Stark. And every bit of intuition she had encouraged her to seek answers.

At last, the computer beeped, announcing its somewhat reluctant readiness to oblige Keira's amateur sleuthing.

Calloway, crime, she plugged in.

And right away, a series of news articles popped up. Keira scrolled through the list. Some were the same as the ones she'd found in Calloway's scrapbook. Some were different.

Home Invasion Gone Wrong? Or Cover-Up Done Right?

Police Seek Husband for Questioning in Gruesome Double Homicide.

Graham Calloway. Doctor. Husband. Stepfather. Killer?

Keira's hand pressed into the stitched-up wound on her leg. A doctor. Well, that explained that.

She sighed, clicked on the last article and began to read.

For Holly Henderson, a fairy-tale romance has ended in tragedy. The twenty-five-year-old (heiress to the Henderson fortune) and her young son were killed in their home nearly one year ago today. It was Dr. Graham Calloway, her estranged husband and the primary beneficiary of the young woman's will, who discovered the murder. Now the police have issued a countrywide manhunt in search of Calloway, who will officially be charged with his wife's and stepson's murders.

Keira read through article after article, piec-
ing together both the murdered woman's life and
her death.

From her teenage years on, Holly was a favorite of the local media. Her late mother was old
money, her father on the rise politically. Holly
herself lived wildly, partying hard and often,
until a surprise pregnancy brought her craziness
to a grinding halt. While quite a bit of scandal
accompanied the announcement, by all reports,
it was the best thing to happen to the young
heiress. After the birth of her son, Holly's name
faded to obscurity, with the only notable events
in the papers being her mother's passing and her
father's election to city councilman. She met and
married her son's pediatrician, Graham Calloway.

Then came the murder.

Keira's heart hammered as she read the details.

The call came in to the 9-1-1 center at two in
the afternoon, and in minutes the police were
on the scene. When the officers got there, they

found Calloway holding his wife's body tightly in one arm, a gun in the other hand.

In spite of the circumstances, Calloway was initially taken at his word. They accepted that he'd found the house and his wife and hadn't called 9-1-1 immediately, but instead tried to revive her. Property damage, missing items, forced entry—all of it pointed to a home invasion gone wrong. But as quickly as the theory was accepted, it began to be discredited. A grieving husband became an angry husband.

And that's when things grew scandalous again.

Calloway became a target, his squeaky-clean reputation dragged through the mud. Troubled, precollege years surfaced. Several articles noted an assault charge at eighteen, and a weapons charge at seventeen. Although the former was pardoned and the latter sealed, somehow each became public knowledge.

The whole marriage was called into question. Calloway reportedly accused Holly of having an affair. A restraining order was said to be in the works. Domestic disturbance calls from the neighbors were rumored. And there were hints at a custody battle over the young boy.

A neighbor came forward, stating she'd heard a noisy argument just minutes before the gunshots. Finally, it was leaked to the press that Holly, who had long ago made Calloway the beneficiary in trust to her massive family fortune, had been about to divert the funds away from her soon-to-be ex-husband.

More and more rumors abounded.

Formal charges were pending.

And then Dr. Graham Calloway disappeared, making every reporter scream about the surety of his guilt.

Keira paused in her reading, wondering why the revelations from the online news sources didn't fill her full of doubt. All she felt was sadness for Calloway. It hurt her heart that he'd lost his family to that kind of violence.

And she was sure that it was something done *to* him, not something done *by* him.

Maybe she could chalk up her conviction to

an inability to accept the truth rather than a gut feeling, but she didn't think so.

Keira looked back to the computer, flipping through the last few articles about the investigation.

The police chased down dozens of leads, followed every rumor. Nothing. They'd chased him countrywide. Assets were frozen, the property and her mother's family's fortune tied up in red tape. Even her politician father couldn't get ahold of a cent.

Eventually, the case was put aside for newer, fresher, solvable ones.

Henry Henderson, Holly's father, catapulted to political stardom.

And Calloway remained at large.

Except he's not at large at all, Keira thought as she leaned away from the computer.

A perfectly capable policeman knew exactly where he was hiding. Where he'd been hiding for years. So why hadn't Officer David Stark turned him in? Somehow, friendship didn't seem to cut it.

Puzzled, Keira punched in Dave's name to the search screen. Unlike Calloway, he had very little digital presence. The usual social media, security settings on high, a mention of community service in the local newspaper and nothing more.

But there *had* to be something more. Some really good reason for not just handing Calloway over to the higher-ups and being done with it.

Keira stared at the screen for a long time, willing herself to see something she'd missed.

Nothing.

She blinked at the computer screen, the words blurring in front of her, and she wondered if it was time to give up, at least for now.

Her finger hovered over the Close Window button.

Keira immediately felt guilty. This wasn't some internet search for cute cat videos. It was a man's innocence. Or guilt. It was his life.

And then an article at the bottom of the screen caught her eye. It didn't have Dave's name in the highlighted link, but the fact that it had popped up in her search struck her as odd.

Paternity Suit Dropped.

Keira brought the pointer down to the article and clicked.

Link not found.

She tried again.

Link not found.

Keira sighed. She rested her chin on her palm, trying to decide if the dead link was even relevant. Irritably, she typed in its title, added a plus sign, then typed Dave's name.

The moment she hit Enter, the computer chose to stall, an evil little circle spinning around on the screen as it took its sweet time thinking about what she'd asked it to look for. It held Keira's sleepy gaze for a good three minutes before her eyes drooped again. Her lids got heavier and heavier, and her shoulders slumped tiredly, and she had to force herself to keep from putting her head down on the keyboard. She could barely make her eyes focus on the information anymore.

She rested her head on the crook of her elbow. *Just for a second*, she thought. *While I wait.* But minutes later, she was sound asleep.

Chapter Twenty

The neighborhood was eerily the same as it had been four years earlier. Though Graham didn't know why he'd expected it to change at all. A lifetime might've passed for him, but it was little more than a blip in the lives of people who lived in these houses with the well-manicured lawns, and the carefully pruned trees and the six-foot-on-the-nose fences. Graham knew, because he'd been one of them not that long ago.

It had seemed ideal. The perfect, ready-made life. So much better than his overpriced bachelor pad in the heart of downtown.

It was Holly—fun, and sassy and a little bit wild—who had brought the neighborhood into

Graham's life. She'd thrown a first birthday party for her son at her inherited house, and even though he didn't usually make social visits to his patients' homes, Graham had felt compelled to go.

In retrospect, it was Holly's cherubic son who drew him in.

And probably who held me there, Graham admitted.

At the party, the little boy had been toddling straight for the in-ground pool in the backyard when Graham spotted him. He'd rushed to the kid's side, grabbing him seconds before he'd plunged in, and just moments after *that*, Holly had latched on to Graham's arm in a rather permanent way.

It was the life Graham had always dreamed of, but struggled to find. His upbringing was hard, his teenage years harsh and lonely, and it had taken every ounce of will to fight his way out. A pretty wife, a perfect son and a nice place to come home to had still seemed far off.

Until that party.

The first thing Graham did when he moved in was to have the pool filled. Which was probably the perfect piece of foreshadowing.

Graham was practical, but Holly liked *nice* things. *Fun* things. *Shiny* things. Things that could hurt Sam, or hurt her, and things that always left Graham wondering just how the hell the package—that perfect-from-the-outside life—could be so different from the contents.

Nothing reminded Graham more of that fact than standing at the end of the street that led into the heart of that neighborhood. Shiny and nice. *False advertising.*

Except for Sam, of course. The kid was heartbreakingly golden. Smart and sweet and full of life. The last part came from Holly, undoubtedly, while the first two were prime examples of the simple ability to overcome the odds. Which Graham related to perfectly. And ultimately, that's what broke him. Not Holly's affairs, or alcohol abuse, or the feeling that he was living on the periphery of some could-have-been life.

Graham wanted that kid. He was willing to

fight for him, tooth and nail, and when Holly finally came out of her boozy haze long enough to realize what was happening, to see that her shiny doctor husband was going to take away her shiny son, she sobered up. Just long enough to kick him out. Just long enough to make him hurt. And just long enough to get killed.

Graham eyed the fork in the road warily.

One direction led to the Niles home and to Keira; the other went straight to Graham's old place and his bad memories.

Funny that he and Keira had lived so close to one another at some point, but never crossed paths.

Though maybe not so funny, if Graham was being honest. The two years he'd called this area home had been a closed-door hell. He hadn't had much time for making new friends. Between putting in sixty hours a week at the clinic, chasing down Holly at every turn and still trying his damnedest to be a good father to Sam.

Graham ran a hand through his shorn hair. As much as the past was to blame for his current predicament, he really didn't have time for dwelling on it.

He planted his feet in the direction of his former life for one moment, then swung toward Keira's parents' house.

Toward my future.

If I have one.

Three blocks brought him to the correct street, and that's where he switched from a comfortable own-the-place swagger to a don't-belong-here skulk. There weren't many people out, but that wasn't terribly surprising. It was noon on a Tuesday, and the residents were mostly at work.

Graham wove through the backyards, grateful for the owners' preference for shared good-neighbor gates and large hedges rather than sparse trees and bolted fences. They offered plenty of cover.

He didn't know what he'd find when he reached the Nileses' place. Maybe Dave would've taken up residence on the couch—a thought that made Graham's lip curl—or maybe he was just watching the place from some panel van on the corner.

Either way, Graham was going to tear a strip off him. The man had jeopardized his hope of keeping Keira alive.

Alive?

That thought didn't just make his lip curl. It didn't even just make him pause. It stopped him dead in his tracks.

He'd been making his plans—a little spontaneous and uncharacteristically reckless—and the resulting moves with the idea of keeping Keira safe. What he *hadn't* been doing was focusing on what it might really mean if he wasn't successful. He hadn't truly considered the fact that her life might be in jeopardy. If she met Michael Ferguson, if Dave somehow put her in contact with him…

Graham closed his hands into fists, flexed them open, then closed them again.

Damn.

Keira would be a witness. She'd become someone who could do something even Graham himself couldn't do—a person who could identify Holly and Sam's murderer on sight. A liability.

No way in hell would the cold-blooded killer let her just walk away at the end of it.

Graham moved a little quicker and he didn't slow again until he was two doors down from the Niles residence.

Once there, he stopped and did a careful visual perusal of the perimeter.

It revealed no sign of his cop friend. There wasn't a single car on the cul-de-sac.

So Dave had either left her alone completely, or Graham's instincts were off and he hadn't brought the girl there at all. A niggling of self-doubt crept in.

What if he was wrong?

Moments later, though, he spied a solitary light in the otherwise-dark Niles home. It was like a tiny beacon from behind the closed blinds, quashing any question Graham had about his gut feeling. He knew he was right; Keira was in there, completely unguarded.

Waiting for him, possibly.

Hopefully.

Graham cut through the final backyard that

lay between him and the girl, then paused on the other side of the fence. After a quick glance around to make sure no one was watching him—at least not overtly—he grabbed ahold of a low-lying branch on a sturdy tree and pulled himself up. He shoved down thoughts of how ridiculous he would seem if caught—*a grown man climbing a neighborhood tree*—and surveyed the Nileses' landscaped yard. It was tidy, but not manicured, well-cared for, but not overdone. A yard *he* might've liked to have when he lived in the area. Holly had been partial to all things marble and all things floral, and with the removal of the pool, had commissioned an elaborate gazebo.

Yard envy is not *the point of this mission*, he reminded himself and moved his gaze around the lot, looking for ways to get to the house without being detected.

A big tree, much like the one where he sat now, offered ample coverage between the edge of the yard and the fence. Just a few feet from that was a line of shrub, a storage shed, then another tree, which was right beside a wide porch.

The layout of the home was familiar to Graham—his had been larger, but otherwise very similar.

The porch hung from the rear of the house. It was topped by a country-style door that undoubtedly led directly into the gourmet kitchen. Glossy wooden steps led up to the second floor. At the top of those was another deck, this one long and narrow. It would be home to sliding glass doors that would lead into the master suite.

And that's your best bet, Graham decided.

He didn't hesitate. He didn't look around as he moved from one spot to the next. If anyone was watching closely enough to catch his stealthy entrance, he didn't want to see them coming. He'd fight, if he had to, but if he was going to be taken out by a sniper, he'd rather not be looking down the barrel of the gun when it happened.

Graham made the transition from one yard to the other easily, and no one stopped him as he sidled up the back stairs. No alarm sounded when he found the sliding glass doors unlocked and slid them open. In fact, the only noise he heard other than his own shallow breaths was a tiny squeak as he slipped from the master suite into the hall.

Careful to tread lightly, Graham eased past the requisite family photos that lined the stairwell. When he hit the middle of the steps, he froze.

There she was, straight across the expansive family room. Her head was down, her face pointed in the other direction, and for a very long, very slow heartbeat, Graham feared the worst. His stomach dropped to his knees, violent waves crashed inside his head and, try as he might, he couldn't breathe.

I'm too late, he thought, an indescribable thrum of desperation weakening his whole body.

His eyes closed and he grabbed at the railing to steady himself, unexpected moisture burning behind his lids.

He sank down to the stairs, racked with despair.

Chapter Twenty-One

Keira had woken with a start, her heart thumping in her chest and her head pressed into her dad's sports-car-themed mouse pad. It only took her a second to remember where she was and why she was there. The only real question was, what had woken her so abruptly?

Her eyes sought the clock above the mantel.

It was 1:03 p.m.

Three hours in a face-plant. And she didn't feel at all refreshed. She rubbed her cheek, trying to smooth out the little marks left by the mouse pad.

Then the ceiling above her squeaked, and she went still.

That's what woke me, she realized.

Keira knew the sound well. The culprits were three loose floorboards, one right outside the master bedroom, one on the very top stair and a final one, three up from the bottom step. When she was a teenager, her dad refused to fix them because there was no way to navigate through the hall without triggering one, making it next to impossible for her to sneak out—or in. Now, her dad said the squeaks added character to the house. But right that second, all they added was fear.

She cursed her own stupidity.

She hadn't bothered to bolt any of the doors or check any of the windows. And someone with good intentions wouldn't sneak in through the upstairs.

Keira glanced to the other side of the room, through the formal dining room to the French doors just off the kitchen. It was the quickest way out. But the back door had a notoriously rusty handle, which often stuck.

Her eyes flicked to the hall at the edge of the living room. It led to the front door. And straight past the stairs—the only way for the intruder to get to her.

She decided to take her chances with the kitchen.

But she waited a second too long. Before she could move, the final squeaky floorboard sounded, and Keira was stuck.

In a panic, she snapped up the nearest thing she could use as a weapon—an egg-shaped marble paperweight—palmed it, then closed her eyes and waited.

She heard the trespasser hit the last step of the stairs softly, then the pause at the bottom. Keira tensed. Whoever was attached to the footfalls didn't come any closer.

Why is he holding back?

She was afraid to breathe. Afraid to move. And her hand, clasped so tightly around the paperweight, was growing sweaty.

Her fingers wanted to move.

They were going to move.

They *did* move.

And even the slight adjustment drew a sharp inhale from her potential attacker.

Dammit.

Keira leaped to her feet, the paperweight slippery in her palm. She zeroed in on the invader.

He was standing on the bottom step. The relative dark created by the tightly drawn blinds obscured his face and bathed it in shadows.

He took a tiny step toward her.

"Stay there!" Keira commanded, only a slight tremor in her voice.

He paused, but only for a second. And Keira wasn't taking any chances. She drew her arm back and prepared to launch the marble egg with all her strength. It might not hit him, he might duck… It didn't matter. What Keira wanted was time.

She tossed the paperweight and turned to run.

He called something after her, but she ignored it.

Go, go, go!

She wasn't anywhere near fast enough. Strong arms closed around her, pinning them to her sides and lifting her from the ground.

"Stop!" His harsh tone not only demanded attention, it required obedience.

She wasn't going to give him the latter, and she was only giving him the former because she had no choice. And she sure as hell wasn't going to make it the *good* kind of attention, either. She kicked her legs, hoping to hit something—anything—important. He just squeezed her tighter.

"Keira!"

She ignored the fact that he knew her name. "Let me *go!*"

He ignored her, too, and backed up until they hit the stairs. He pulled her to a sitting position, his thick, muscular thighs wide around her, hugging her hips snuggly.

Keira wanted to yell, to holler for help, but her throat was dry, and she was scared that a scream might prompt him to do something worse than whatever he was already planning.

A little moan escaped from her lips. "Please."

"Keira."

Her name, the second time, was spoken much

more softly. And finally she recognized the voice.

"Calloway," she whispered, her whole body sagging with relief.

"It's me," he murmured into her hair.

For a second, Keira just let herself lean against him, appreciative of his solidity. But it didn't take long for the heat in her body to rise. It bloomed from each part of Calloway's body that touched her. His inner thighs to her outer thighs. The bottom of his forearms on the top of hers and his chest pressed into her back. Her rear end pushed straight into his—

With an embarrassed gasp, Keira pulled herself away.

Clearly, all it took was the feel of his body against hers to turn her blood into lava and her mind into mush.

Which isn't so bad...is it?

"What are you doing here? You said two days. You're okay?" she made herself ask, trying to calm the blood rushing through her system and failing completely as she took in his changed appearance.

Dr. Graham Calloway.

The title seemed at odds with the man she'd met in the woods, but at that moment, she had no problems imagining him in the role. He'd shaved his beard, revealing a strong jaw and showcasing those amazing lips of his. The clean-cut look suited him and took years off his face. A white T-shirt hugged his thick, well-muscled body, and a pair of slightly too-big jeans hung a little low on his hips. He sat on the step above her, the extra height making him look even bigger than usual. From where Keira was, she had to tip her head up to meet his gaze.

God, he looks good.

He brought his hand up to push back his hair and gave her a clear view of his gray eyes. The want in them burned brightly. Keira's pulse thrummed even harder.

"Will a sliding scale do?" Calloway wondered out loud, and Keira had to struggle to remember what question she'd asked him in the first place.

"Sure," she managed to get out.

He tipped his head to one side thoughtfully. "All right. Three out of ten for having a hard object thrown at my head. Eight out of ten for having found you alive. Two out of ten because I'm a little disappointed that you're finally wearing pants."

Keira blushed, jumped to her feet and smoothed the borrowed pajama bottoms. "Are you just going to sit there?"

"Did you have something else in mind?" he teased.

Keira shook off the innuendo—and what it did to her—and headed straight for the kitchen without turning to see if he followed.

GRAHAM WATCHED KEIRA walk away, just because it was a nice view. He waited until she'd fully disappeared down the hall before he rose to follow her.

He felt markedly different now that he knew she was okay. Almost relaxed. He knew it was a bit—*okay, a lot*—premature to be letting down his guard, but for some reason, he couldn't quite help it. Seeing Keira in her own element probably had something to do with it. Even though it wasn't *her* home, it was a home she was clearly comfortable in.

Silently, she filled a kettle. She skirted the island with familiarity, rummaged through the cupboards, found what she was looking for, then set up two mismatched cups with chamomile tea bags. She didn't speak as she worked, but Graham had no problem imagining her humming as she went along, pulling out some kind of loaf from the freezer, thawing it in the microwave, then setting that on the counter beside the tea.

It was nice. Normal. Graham liked it.

So he stayed quiet, too, waiting as she laid everything out. When she was done, he took a small sip of the tea and let the floral flavor lie on his tongue for a moment before swallowing.

Keira climbed onto an island stool beside him, her knee almost touching his. Her delicate hands wrapped her mug, and she shot him an expectant look.

Graham wished immediately that the meeting wasn't about to take a serious turn. He wanted to make her blush again and laugh. He wanted to kiss those lips and drag that hair from its tight ponytail and forget that they were in any kind of danger.

But you can't.

There were other far more pressing matters to deal with. He needed to ask her why Dave had brought her here instead of staying in the resort town. And why he'd left her alone. When he opened his mouth, though, something else entirely came out.

"I'd like to turn that sliding scale into a ten out of ten."

"What—"

Graham didn't let her finish. He put one hand on the back of her head and the other on her chin. She trembled a little in her seat, but she remained glued to the spot as Graham lifted her face gently and kissed her lips. And as light as his touch was, desire surged through him.

Slow it down, Graham cautioned himself.

He trailed a finger down her cheek, then leaned back and smiled.

"Eight," he joked. "Maybe nine."

There was that blush.

Damn.

He drew her close again. He dragged his mouth down her cheek, tracing the curve of it, and the pink spread from her face to her throat. Then lower. He pulled away so he could look at her, so he could admire the arch of her brow and the swell of her breast and see that she wanted him as badly as he wanted her. He wasn't disappointed. Keira's lids were half-closed, and what little he could see of her eyes was glossy with heat. Her chest rose and fell against his enticingly.

To hell with slow.

Graham's grip on her neck tightened, and she gasped. He pulled her forcefully into his lap, making her teeter a bit on his knee, her legs dangling down. Her choice was between holding him tightly and falling to the ground. Thankfully, she chose the former. Her arms slid up to Graham's neck while his arms slipped to her waist.

He kissed her again. Forcefully. Possessively. She opened her mouth, welcoming his exploration. Her hands were in his hair and then they were sliding down his back, then holding him as if he was her lifeline.

"Graham," she said against his mouth, and he liked the way his name sounded on her lips.

"Yes, love?" he breathed back.

"I'm scared."

Fierce protectiveness filled his heart.

"I won't let anyone hurt you," he promised, and he meant it. *Not as long as I'm alive.*

Keira shook her head slowly. "No. I'm not scared for me."

"What're you scared for?"

"You. And us. If there *is* one, I mean. Or could be. I don't want this to be it."

Graham heard the need in her voice, and he had a matching one—an almost painful one—in his own when he answered. "I like you, Keira. More than like you. I have since the second I saw you in that car. That's the real, selfish reason I pulled you out. I wanted to know you. As crazy as it is, I felt like I *had* to. Or maybe I felt a little like I already did. The line is kind of blurred. I don't know if I can promise you a future—hell, maybe that's not even what you're asking—but I can give you now. I can give you honesty. I can give you *us*."

Her eyes were wide and hopeful. "All right."

Trust, unexpected and almost unbelievable, expanded in Graham's chest.

"I'm not a perfect man," he warned her.

"I know," she replied.

Graham grinned. "Oh, you do, do you?"

She went pink. "I meant I don't *expect* you to be perfect."

When in doubt, go for shock.

"I lit your car on fire," Graham stated.

Keira face went a little redder. "I know that, too."

Graham raised an eyebrow.

"Dave told me," Keira admitted.

"Did he tell you *why*?"

"To cover up the evidence. But he meant it in a bad way. I know better."

Graham swallowed. His throat was raw with appreciation of her understanding, but his heart was dark with guilt at needing it.

"How do *you* think I meant it?" he asked.

"You were buying time. Protecting yourself."

"I don't know if you know this, Keira, but most men don't commit a felony in the name of self-preservation." He was half joking, but she didn't smile.

"I'm glad you're not most men," she said.

He leaned in to give her a soft kiss. "Did Dave tell you anything else about me?"

"Not really."

"But?" Graham pushed.

"I searched you on Google."

"I'll bet *that* didn't have anything nice to say about me."

"I don't believe everything I read."

"But some of it?"

"Not most of it."

Graham closed his eyes for a long moment, but

he could still feel Keira's gaze on him. It wasn't judgmental or even assessing. Just patient. She put a hand on his cheek.

"You can tell me," she said.

Graham opened his eyes and nodded. "Holly was wild. Impetuous. A little crazy, sometimes. Her mom died when she was young—just nineteen—and left her a lot of money. Her dad was never able to control her and, believe me, he tried. Screened her boyfriends, put a tracking device on her car, recorded her phone calls, you name it. But she was an adult. At least in the strictest sense of the word. She refused to be reined in. She wasn't even trying. It's just who she was. The baby—Sam—slowed her down for a while. But as soon as she was settled, as soon as *I* was settled…she started up again. Drinking and other men…"

"It's not your fault," Keira said, sounding very sure.

Graham was sure, too. Holly *couldn't* be controlled, and it had nothing to do with Graham.

That didn't stop him from feeling guilty about her death.

The truth.

"I didn't love her." The admission came out hoarse, and Graham cleared his throat and tried again. "I didn't love her, but I was a good husband. A faithful husband. And that kid… I loved him more than I've loved anyone before or since." His voice was rough once more, and this time he let it stay that way. "I couldn't let anyone think I had anything to do with his murder. I'd rather die myself. That's why I ran. Why I paid Dave to search for the man who killed them. Why I've never been able to walk away and start fresh, even though I've got the means." He looked at her face and saw the tears threatening to overflow, and his heart broke a little more. "I'm sorry, Keira—"

Her lips cut him off. Her fingers dug in to his hair, then ran smoothly, soothingly, over the back of his neck. She was pouring herself into the kiss, and Graham accepted it. Reluctantly at first, but with increased acceptance. Then with enthusiasm. He met her attention forcefully, his tongue finding purchase between her lips, his hands getting lost in her auburn tresses. She sank into his arms. She belonged there. When she pulled away, Graham felt the loss all over.

Then she spoke, and the loss was forgotten.

"My bedroom is upstairs," she said, her words loaded with promise. "Third door on the left."

Wordlessly, Graham scooped her up and moved at double time to the staircase.

Chapter Twenty-Two

They were a tangled mess of arms and legs and bedsheets and sweat. Calloway's muscular, over-size body took up three quarters of the available space. Never before had Keira's double bed in her childhood room seemed so small.

But it's the perfect size, too, she thought as she opened her sleepy eyes and looked over at him.

His face was still peaceful, and Keira was a little envious. A silly grin was plastered on her own. And her mind refused to sit still because it was too full of sweet nothings.

Beautiful.

Incredible.

Amazing.

And the way he said her name. The way he whispered it. The way he called it out, as if there was no one else in the world.

And what he'd said earlier was right. It *was* crazy to feel like this. It would be crazy to feel like this even after a few months. But after only a few days… That pushed it right over the edge. But damned if Keira cared.

She examined his face carefully, memorizing the lines of it in the soft morning light. She liked the thick crest of his eyebrows and the dusting of silver in his hair. Already, the shadow of a beard peppered his cheeks. She liked that, too.

Her heart wanted to burst through her chest with its fullness.

But there was a heaviness there, too. One the allover glow couldn't quite mask.

Because Calloway wasn't safe, and their time together was finite. His hideaway was no longer an option, her parents' house wasn't any better and her own apartment was the first place the man who'd killed Calloway's family would look.

Their only option was to run somewhere else.

"No."

Calloway's statement was soft but decisive. And he hadn't even opened his eyes.

"No, what?" Keira replied.

"I can feel you thinking."

"Someone else's thinking can't be felt," she argued.

He cracked one lid. "Yours can."

Keira made a weak effort to detangle herself from his arms, but he held her firmly in place. She didn't struggle too hard. Truthfully, she was happier to rest her head against him than she was to resist him.

"I didn't even know you were awake," she said as she trailed her palm across his chest.

"Little hard to stay asleep while you're plotting something that's going to kill you."

"That isn't what I was doing."

Calloway eased his hold and rolled both of them to their sides, so they were facing each other.

"No?" he said. "What *were* you thinking about, then?"

"Leaving."

"Leaving?" he repeated, sounding surprised.

"Leaving together," she clarified. "You don't have to find Ferguson. Or risk *your* life. Not if we run."

"Keira…"

"They already think I'm dead," she reminded him. "Dave told me the media was all over the story."

Calloway's expression clouded. "And you're just going to walk away and let it stay that way?"

A lump formed in Keira's throat. "They'll mourn and move on."

"How long will you last? What if one of *them* dies? Will you stay away when they have the funeral? Or one of your parents gets sick or has an accident?" He shook his head, then added in a harsh voice, "You have no idea what you're saying. What you're committing to."

"I don't see what other choice I have."

"You can stay here, and let your family and friends know you're alive."

"And what happens to you?"

He smoothed her hair back from her face. "Are you asking what happens to *me*, or what happens to that *us* we talked about?"

Keira didn't answer him. She *was* worried about Calloway directly. She didn't want the police to catch him or for him to be arrested for a crime he hadn't committed. But she also had to admit—at least to herself—that she was scared of losing him. She was just too embarrassed to make the declaration out loud.

Two short days, and you need this man as badly as you need air.

Even thinking it was enough to make her face heat up.

When she stayed silent, Calloway sighed. "I've spent a long time isolated from the people I knew. It nearly killed me to hear the rumors. It nearly broke me a hundred times. Hiding is the hardest damned thing I've ever done. I would never forgive myself for dragging you into that life."

"I don't care," Keira said, her voice full of residual post-lovemaking conviction.

"You *think* you don't care."

"Don't tell me what I think."

"I wouldn't dare."

Calloway leaned forward and gave her bottom lip a little tug with his teeth. Then he released it and ran a hand over the same spot, sending renewed sparks of desire through her. Keira stifled a pleasure-filled sigh. Calloway's face was determined, his jaw set and his eyes not in the slightest bit tired. And Keira had the distinct feeling that he was trying to distract her. He formed a lazy path from her mouth to her shoulder to her hip, then traced a circle over her sheet-covered abdomen.

Two more seconds of that *and it's going to work.*

Keira grabbed his hand, determined herself. She needed to make him understand that she wasn't going to just let him slip away. He tried to pull his hand out of hers. She held firm. *Take that.* But his thumb was still loose, and it began to move up and down, just below her belly button, and it was far more distracting than his whole palm had been.

She willed herself not to give in to the temptation he presented.

"You've been gone for a long time," she said. "So maybe you've forgotten how to compromise. Relationships are a two-way street, Calloway."

He didn't even blink at her use of the *R* word. "What do you want me to do, Keira? Let Dave take me in? Say the word, and that's what will happen. But there is absolutely zero chance of me allowing you to abandon your life on my behalf."

Keira's stomach dropped. "You can't go to jail."

"I will, if it means keeping you safe."

"I'm not letting you sacrifice yourself for me any more than you're letting me sacrifice myself for you!"

In an unexpected move, Calloway flipped her from her side to her back, then propped himself above her, his biceps flexing with the effort.

"You're a stubborn girl, aren't you?"

"No."

"That blush tells me you *know* you're a stubborn girl," he teased. "I *have* to prove my innocence, Keira. Or we don't stand a chance. Do you know where Dave went?"

"He said he had to take care of a few things." She paused. "Calloway…"

"Yes?"

Keira pulled the sheet over her chest, then propped herself on her elbow, facing him. "Why would he suddenly start thinking you're guilty?"

Calloway's expression clouded with surprise. "Is that what he said?"

"Not exactly. It's what he implied. Or maybe what I inferred. But it was like he was trying to scare me."

"But he *knows* I'm innocent," Calloway muttered.

"He knows it?"

Calloway gave her tight nod. "Dave's the one who found Holly. Hours before I got home."

Keira frowned. "But the papers said it was *you* who found her."

He ran his fingers over the ridges in her forehead. "I thought you didn't believe everything you read."

"I don't. But that's a pretty big discrepancy."

"Lie down with me again."

Keira opened her mouth to tell him no, they had more important things to worry about. But when she caught the pleading look in his eyes, she was powerless to resist. She curled up beside him, her body tucked beside his, her head resting on his chest.

GRAHAM WAITED UNTIL Keira was settled, the soft scent of her hair flooding his senses, calming the thud of his heart.

"If you want to listen, I'll tell you the story," he said, his voice low.

"Okay," she agreed.

And for the first time, he told the full truth, and shared the hard thoughts that kept him awake for four years.

"Dave and I met in high school. We started out hating each other. We fought, actually, in one of those parking-lot fights, with the crowd of guys egging us on and screaming for blood. God knows what it was about. We both got suspended. Not a first for me, but Dave's dad was a cop, and he was royally pissed off that I was ruining his kid's life. He turned up at my house, demanding to know what *I* had done. When he saw my living situation, well, I guess he took pity on me. Absentee mom. Drunk dad. So instead of giving me hell, he took me home and commanded Dave to take care of me." Graham paused and laughed as he remembered it.

Dave's father was everything Dave wasn't. Hard and decisive on the outside, kind and insightful on the inside. He didn't take anyone's garbage. Graham admired him. Loved him.

"He changed my life," Graham told Keira, curling a strand of her hair around one of his fingers. "He gave me value. Helped me get that scholarship for med school and made me believe I could do it. He died when we were twenty, and I promised him I'd see it through. He even left me a bit of money to help out. But Dave took his death badly, and pretty soon it was me carrying his weight instead of the other way around. Sorting out his fights and saving his rear end every weekend. If it hadn't been for his father's name, I doubt he would ever have made it past the first day as a policeman. He developed a hell of a gambling problem and I was always bailing him out of one debt or another. We went on like that for years, Dave messing up and me picking up the pieces."

"Just like you did with Holly," Keira added.

"Just like that," Graham agreed, then took a thick breath. "Which brings me to the next bit. Things moved fast for Holly and me. Met and married in less than a year. I adopted Sam…and Holly adopted Dave."

"They had an affair?" Keira asked.

"There were things…a pattern, I guess, that took me a while to notice. Money moved from her account on the same day he paid off a car he could never afford in the first place. Every time Holly made a cash withdrawal, Dave would show up with something newer and shinier. A suit. A computer. A vacation in the Bahamas. And he stopped asking *me* for money. Holly got more and more distant. And once, I overheard a very heated conversation between the two of them. Holly was yelling about jealousy and entitlement, and Dave was yelling back about sharing what should never have been mine."

"But you never asked either of them if your suspicion was true?"

Graham shook his head. "I rationalized *not* asking. What if I was wrong? I didn't want to ruin nearly a decade and a half of friendship. Or worse, jeopardize what I had with Sam. So I just started the divorce process on the sly. I hired the best lawyer I could afford, who promptly figured out that we were near to broke. My income and our assets were the only thing keeping us afloat. All of Holly's savings were gone, her investments mostly sold off, her cards maxed out. Which meant I had no choice but to confront her. But I never even got as far as asking about Dave before she flipped out. She threw everything I owned out on the street. Then threw me out, too. Three days later, the cops were at my hotel room door. Holly had drunk herself into a stupor, fallen down the stairs and called 9-1-1, blaming *me*. For the first time in a long time, Dave had to come to my aid. He bailed me out, dropped me off, then went to reason with Holly. Instead… Well, you know what he found."

"That's terrible." Keira's voice was full of the same ache that plagued Graham's heart, but then she spoke again, and her tone was also puzzled. "Why didn't he just report it himself?"

"I told him not to," Graham admitted. "I thought I was protecting him. And what was left of Holly's reputation."

"And that's why he helped you all these years?"

"Yes."

Keira pushed herself up and met Graham's eyes. "But, if he just admitted that he was there first, wouldn't that exonerate you?"

Graham shrugged. "Exonerate? No. Create reasonable doubt? Maybe. Or it might just implicate Dave, and as much as I question his motives at the moment...he's not a killer."

"You know that for sure?"

"I believe it one hundred percent."

"So we're back to wondering why he suddenly changed his mind about you being the good guy."

Graham stared at her pinched-up features and couldn't suppress a smile.

"Is that where we are?" he teased. "I thought we were in bed, getting ready to—"

She cut him off. "I'm going to ask him."

Graham's grin fell off his face immediately. "No."

"Are you telling me what to do again, Mountain Man?"

"This time, yes, I am. Do *not* ask Dave Stark why he changed his mind about protecting me."

"Asking him is the only thing that makes sense," Keira argued. "And you're supposed to be chasing after Ferguson."

"You take priority, Keira. I'll deal with Dave first," Graham said grimly. "He owes me an explanation for what he said to you, and for leaving you here alone."

She opened her mouth as if she was going to protest again, then closed it and laid her head back on his chest.

"Calloway?" she said after a minute.

"Yes?"

He braced himself for another spiel about how and why she should endanger herself. Instead, her fingernail traced his collarbone, then his pectoral muscles, then found the edge of the sheet, just below his waistline.

"What were you saying before?"

"About?" The word came out throaty and full of heat.

Now her hand slipped *under* the sheet.

"About what we were getting ready to do in this bed," she filled in.

With a growl that made her laugh, Graham grabbed her by the hips and lifted her over top of him.

Chapter Twenty-Three

Keira eyed Calloway guiltily. He was definitely sleeping this time, his handsome face slack, his breathing even.

Seduction had never been Keira's strong point, but she'd worked her hardest to wear him out.

Not that it wasn't rewarding for her, as well. Graham was a fierce and attentive lover. And that made her feel even worse.

But there's no way he'll willingly let you out of his sight, she reminded herself.

She felt that little tug at her heart again, pleased that he cared so much. He'd be mad when he woke up and found out she was gone. Furious, probably. But it was worth it, if she could figure out what it was that Dave was after. Because she had a feeling it was more than misguided morals and Keira felt just as protective of Calloway as he did of her. His story broke her heart. She couldn't help but wonder how much of *his* heart remained in pieces, as well. Every time he said his stepson's name, she heard the pain.

I want to fix that.

She knew justice wouldn't make Calloway whole immediately, but maybe it would start the healing process.

Keira slid her body free from Calloway's embrace, stood up and stepped to the closet. A stack of board games and her mother's rejects—the clothes she couldn't wear anymore but refused to part with—greeted her.

Keira snagged an oversize T-shirt and a pair of leggings, and reminded herself that she wasn't trying to impress Dave with her fashion sense anyway. That didn't stop her from cringing at her appearance as she caught sight of her reflection in the mirror on the back of the door.

Her hair was a disaster, and the wound on her thigh, though held together nicely by Graham's stitches, was still hideous.

She slid on the clothes and patted her hair. Now she looked as if she'd dressed up as her mother for Halloween.

"Nice," she muttered aloud before she remembered she was supposed to be keeping quiet.

Calloway stirred, letting out a noisy sigh, and Keira froze, her eyes fixed to his image in the mirror.

Do not *wake up*, she commanded silently.

He rolled to his side and stretched one arm up, and the bedsheet slid down, revealing a tantalizing amount of skin. Keira's eyes roamed the exposed flesh greedily for a second before she gave herself a mental kick in the butt and opened the door, cutting off her view.

She moved into the hall, wincing as the first telltale floorboard squeaked. But there was no sound from the bedroom, so she moved on to the stairs.

She went still when a loud knock on the back door reached her ears. Then she heard it squeal open.

What the heck?

With her heart in her throat, Keira tiptoed down the stairs and paused outside the kitchen. Part of her wanted to charge in and tackle who-ever was in there. Part of her wanted to wake Calloway for protection.

She steeled herself not to do either.

After all, home invaders didn't usually knock before they let themselves in. Did they?

Her assumption was confirmed when a familiar voice called out, "Keira?"

Drew.

What was he doing here? He wasn't supposed to be back from his business trip yet.

She had to get rid of him before he figured out that Calloway was in the house.

Keira took a breath and stepped into the kitchen. She fixed what she hoped was a sur-prised—and not guilty—look on her face as she greeted him.

"Drew! Where did you come from? How did you even know I was here? You scared the heck out of me!"

He immediately wrapped his arms around her. "*I* scared *you*? Thank God you're okay!"

She extracted herself from his embrace, marveling at the fact that just a few days ago, she'd been considering pursuing a relationship with this man. She didn't feel the remotest bit of attraction toward him.

"Why wouldn't I be okay?" she asked.

Drew fixed her with a concerned gaze. "Your face is plastered all over the news, Keira."

"Is it?"

He raised a speculative eyebrow, and Keira told herself she needed to rein in the innocence a bit.

"They said you'd been in a horrible accident on the mountain. That your car went over the side of some cliff."

They'd identified her.

This is bad.

Did that mean that Dave Stark had given his

official statement, or had his plan been circum-
vented?

Or is he the one that leaked her name?

Drew closed his hand on her elbow. "Hey. You
still with me?"

Keira shook her head and moved away. "I'm
fine. I just—I was about to sneak out for a quick
cup of coffee. You want to come?"

Drew frowned as if he wanted to say no, and
for a second she hoped he would. But then his
eyes fixed on something just over her shoulder,
and Keira followed his gaze to the spot where
she and Calloway had abandoned their mugs
earlier. Her pulse jumped.

"You sure you want coffee? Looks like you
already had some tea for two," Drew observed.

She forced a laugh. "I guess I was a bit tired
this morning when I got in. I made a cup, forgot about it, made another, then didn't drink either of them."

"So you didn't have company?"

"Company?" Keira echoed nervously.

Drew nudged her shoulder. "You know. A

guest. Like me, but who doesn't know where your parents keep the extra key to the back door."

Keira shook her head. "No guests. Unless you're *actually* counting yourself. So...coffee?"

Drew nodded, and Keira breathed a big sigh of relief as he held the door open. She followed him out, careful not to let her eyes stray toward her bedroom window.

When Graham woke, he reached for Keira automatically. As though he'd been waking up beside her for years instead of days.

But a lot can happen in days, he thought drowsily. *You can lose a life. Start a new one. Fall in love. Become something you never thought you'd be.*

His hand slid across the bed, already anticipating the silky feel of her skin under his palm. When his expectation fell through, his eyes flew open. Her spot on the bed was decidedly empty.

Graham sat up and swung his bare legs to the floor.

"Keira?"

He waited about ten seconds for her to answer, and when she didn't, he grew irrationally worried.

"Keira!" he called a bit louder.

He snapped up his jeans and T-shirt from the floor, slipped them on without bothering to locate his discarded underwear, and moved toward the door. He cracked it open and paused. The house was ominously silent.

"Hey!"

He made his way downstairs, taking the steps two at a time. The sun was going down, and the main floor was nearly dark. Worse than that, there was no sign of Keira.

Where the hell had she gone?

He stepped from the bottom of the stairs to the kitchen and flicked on the lights. The two nearly full mugs of chamomile tea still sat where they'd left them.

Dread was pooling rather quickly in Graham's gut.

He walked around the kitchen slowly, trying

to find a clue that would give him a hint as to where she'd disappeared to.

And whether or not it had been on purpose. Or for that matter...purposeful.

"She could've just needed something from the store," Graham told himself out loud.

The thought eased his mind for a tenth of a second. Then a little white card on the edge of the counter caught his eye.

He lifted it slowly.

"Sergeant David Stark," it read, followed by a phone number in bold.

"Well, that answers that," he muttered.

No wonder she'd dropped the whole ask-Dave issue so easily. She'd already made the decision to disobey Graham's request.

Did you really expect her to obey *you?*

She'd been nothing but a challenge since the second he pulled her from the wreck. Which he liked. Except right at that second. Graham gritted his teeth. Right that second, what he wished was that she was a complacent pushover waiting for him to make the decisions so he could keep her safe.

He paced the length of the kitchen, then out to the living room, then back again, trying—and failing—to find an outlet for his frustration.

He cursed himself for being played as much as he cursed her for playing him.

And play you she did. Like a damned drum.

Of course, his body had been more than happy to let her have her way with him. She fit in his arms so perfectly, it was as if she was made for him. And when she fixed those green eyes on him, her pupils dilated with need, her mouth parted slightly as she exhaled his name…

Graham shook his head. That kind of passion wasn't a ploy. That kind of chemistry couldn't be faked. So, yeah, she might've been manipulating him with sex, but she hadn't been immune to what was happening between them. He was sure of it.

Graham paused on his third run through the living room and ran his fingers through his hair.

It really wasn't nearly as satisfying as it had been when it was still long.

He needed something to *do*. Something to occupy his mind and his hands. His eyes flicked around the room until they found the dimly lit computer in the corner.

It had been a very long time since Graham had used a computer. His brief search on the trucker's phone was the closest he'd come to that kind of technology since he went into hiding.

Keira looked you up. It's only fair that you look her up in return.

He smiled a self-satisfied smile. He was pretty damned sure she'd hate the thought of being checked up on.

DREW SET DOWN a paper cup in front of Keira. It was chocolate-and-coffee scented and topped with a generous dollop of whipped cream.

"Decaf mocha," he said. "I know it's your favorite."

"Thanks." Keira took a sip, grateful for the

way the hot liquid warmed her and for the extra second it gave her to gather her thoughts.

Drew waited patiently as she slurped off the whipped cream. He didn't deserve to be lied to the way she was going to have to lie to him. Another tickle of guilt rubbed at Keira's mind. She covered it with a second mouthful of mocha.

Guilt, fear and desire. Those three things seemed to have dominated her emotions since the second she laid eyes on Graham Calloway.

Drew finally broke the too-long silence. "You want to tell me what happened up there on the mountain?"

She met his gaze from across the table.

He really did know her well. Maybe better than anyone except her closest girlfriends. He'd been a shoulder for her on a few occasions, a great help to her parents on many more. And right that moment, she was selfishly tempted to tell him the truth, even if just to garner his opinion on what to do.

She opened her mouth and then closed it.

It's not your secret to tell.

And letting the metaphorical cat out of the bag would only ease the pressure of keeping it under wraps temporarily. It would expose Calloway in a way that Keira would never forgive herself for.

"I don't really remember what happened," Keira lied softly.

Drew frowned. "You don't remember?"

"I remember the crash. And the cop who drove me home. Everything between is kind of fuzzy."

"The cop who picked you up…did he say anything else about what happened up there?" Drew pushed.

"Like what?"

"Like the fact that when they were searching for you, they found some abandoned cabin that might've belonged to an accused murderer. That before that cop found you, they thought maybe the killer had got to you. They even issued some kind of manhunt just in case."

Keira's vision blurred for a dizzying second and she reached for the table to steady herself. She swallowed, her throat dry. She drank some more of the mocha. It did nothing to ease her parched mouth, and the rush of blood to her head wasn't letting up, either.

Was it a coincidence, or had Dave Stark taken his betrayal of Calloway a step further and exposed him to the press?

Oh, God. Are they still looking for him?

"Keira?"

"I'm okay," she managed to get out.

"You sure?"

"Yeah. I guess the thought of being that close to a suspected killer… What else did the news say about the alleged murder?"

"Alleged? This guy—Graham Calloway—has been on the run for years. If he was innocent, something would've turned up by now. You know, they never even found the kid's body? And apparently he stole some thirty-million-dollar painting from his wife before he killed her."

"He…" Keira trailed off, her thoughts suddenly a jumbled mess. "Did they say all of that on the news?"

"Online."

"I didn't read anything like that. He didn't—" Keira snapped her mouth shut.

"Who didn't do what?"

Dammit. She needed to get ahold of herself. Her tongue seemed to be working faster than her brain. She had to fix that.

"The cop," she said slowly. "He didn't say anything about any of that."

"What *did* he say?"

"To keep to myself. In fact, he'd probably be pretty annoyed with me if he knew I was out in public."

"I bet he would."

"What?"

"It's frustrating when you give someone instructions and they don't listen."

Keira sensed something ominous in his words, but she couldn't pinpoint her worry, so she lifted the mocha up and covered her concern with a gulp.

"I should take you home, I think. Wouldn't want to anger that cop," Drew stated.

Keira nodded, the bobbing motion making her

head feel funny. Really funny. Weirder than it had since she'd first banged it in the car accident.

She stood up, bumping the table and sloshing around her mocha. She made a move to grab it, but Drew was quicker.

"You've probably had enough of that," he said.

That struck Keira as funny, and a tinny giggle escaped her lips. "Enough decaf mocha?"

"Mmm-hmm."

Drew slid an arm around her waist and clasped her elbow, then led her from the café to the street. It felt wrong to be in someone else's arms. But she didn't have the energy to pull away. Not even when she noted—rather vaguely—that they were heading in the wrong direction. They walked along in silence, Drew keeping Keira from stumbling, and Keira trying to grasp the elusive warning bells that kept sounding in her head.

They rang even louder as Drew paused in front of an older sedan.

"This isn't your car," she pointed out lamely.

"No," he agreed. "It's not. This car belongs to someone else."

"Who?" Keira wasn't even sure why she asked.

"Mike Ferguson."

A violent shiver wracked Keira's body.

Mike Ferguson. Calloway's *Mike Ferguson. The killer.*

"I don't think I know him," Keira lied.

"Don't worry. You're about to get to know him quite well, actually."

Keira met Drew's eyes, and they didn't look like his eyes at all.

In fact, the man she thought she knew—the one who'd been her parents' neighbor for nearly half a decade, who always had something nice to say about her clothes or her hair, and who mowed her dad's lawn *just so* when they were on vacation—was gone.

If Keira bumped into a man who looked like this in a dark alley, she'd run screaming in the other direction. She wanted to run screaming *now.* But when she moved her legs, they turned to jelly and the sidewalk wobbled. Drew caught her.

"I've thought a lot about what I would do if

you ever fell into my arms, Keira," he said, his voice as dark as his expression. "It's unfortunate that it ended up being like *this*."

Keira flailed a little, but all she did was send herself into the side of the sedan. Her hips smacked the door handle hard enough to bring tears to her eyes. Drew's grip tightened.

"You should really be more careful."

"I'm careful," she said, her words slurred. "Usually."

"Not careful enough. Not today anyway." His voice dropped low as he went on. "If some killer *had* found you, and he *did* follow you here, he wouldn't have too much trouble getting in. What if that happened?"

"Alleged," Keira corrected, smacking her lips in an attempt to fend off the numbness that seemed to be overtaking her mouth.

"I'm not talking about Graham Calloway now, Keira."

"Who *are* you talking about?"

Drew smiled.

He smiled.

And it was a terrible smile that bared his teeth and turned his face hard. A smile that said, "Me." *Oh, God.*

GRAHAM PULLED OUT the chair, straddled it and gave the mouse another click. In minutes, he'd had Keira's name plugged in. Except his search had been almost fruitless. Only two things popped up—a link to her social media and a brief mention in a local paper.

After a swift perusal of the first, and a read-through of the second, he felt as if a few hours with her had taught him more than the virtual world ever could.

So much for the magic of Google.

Then Graham frowned. Hadn't she said Dave told her that her accident was all over the news?

He tapped the keyboard again.

Keira Niles. Car accident.

Nothing.

Keira Niles. Rocky Mountains.

Even less than nothing.

Car crash, Rocky Mountain Resort.

Nope.

Maybe his search was too broad. Maybe her story hadn't reached anything national yet.

Graham racked his brain as he tried to recall the name of the local paper.

Derby Reach Gazette?

He typed it in and the computer autocorrected it to Derby Reach Post, and Graham added her name once more.

"Nothing," he muttered to the empty room. "What the hell is going on? I know she wasn't *lying.*"

He was as sure of that as he was of the fact that her feelings for him weren't phony. So if she'd been telling the truth... Graham's fierce worry came back, stronger than before.

He pushed the chair back and, two seconds too late, realized he wasn't alone in the house anymore.

"Dave was the one lying to her," he said.

As if on cue, Dave's voice came from behind him. "I'll tell you what you want to know, Graham, if you agree to come with me.

Graham jumped to his feet two seconds too late and spun, prepared to throw a punch straight into his disloyal friend's face.

Unfortunately, the other man had a pistol levelled at his chest.

For a long moment, Graham stared at the weapon and seriously considered whether or not to jump him anyway. He took a step in the other man's direction, and Dave cocked the pistol.

"I wouldn't move again," Dave cautioned. "Not suddenly anyway."

"Are you really going to shoot me, Dave?" Graham demanded coolly.

"I'd prefer not to," the other man replied. "But I'll kneecap you if I have to."

"What *do* you want, then?

"The same thing you do. To make sure Keira Niles is safe."

Graham shot Dave a disbelieving look. "You've got a funny way of showing it."

The policeman made an exasperated noise. "I've done everything I can. I took her off the mountain. I gave her strict instructions to stay home. I'm here now to—"

Graham cut him off. "Where is she?"

Surprise registered on Dave's face. "She's not here?"

"I thought she was with you."

"Me? Why would she be with me?"

"Because she wanted to ask you why you stopped helping me. Because she's stubborn as hell. Because I found *your* business card on the counter, and now she's gone."

"I wish she *had* called," Dave replied with a headshake. "She was supposed to, if you happened to walk through the front door."

"I didn't come through the front door," Graham muttered. "Where is she, Dave?"

The policeman lifted the gun and used it to scratch his forehead. "Motivation."

"What?"

"Mike Ferguson's guy…he must've followed us. Stupid of me, I guess. I took the man at his word."

Graham's blood ran cold. "You're actually working with him."

Dave didn't respond to the accusation.

"I'll take you to Keira," he offered instead. "But I'm going to need you to put on my cuffs."

Graham snorted derisively. "Like hell."

"We don't have time to fight about this."

"Then give me the gun." Graham shrugged. "Why would I even believe you know where she is?"

"What's the alternative here, Graham? You think I'm going to have you slap on the cuffs so I can drag you to *jail*? Think about that for just one second. Your rear end is *my* rear end. If I turn you in, it'll either come out that I've been helping you, and the justice system will take me down, or it *won't* come out, and Ferguson will take me down instead. At least this way, we both stand a chance." Dave paused and used his free hand to pull a set of handcuffs from his pocket. "I know that the second I let down my guard, you'll beat the hell out of me."

"I'll beat the hell out of you if I even *think* you're letting your guard down."

Dave sighed. "Cuffs, Graham?"

Graham grabbed them from the other man's outstretched hand. He held them for a second, feeling the rift between the importance of his past and the importance of his present widening. If he put them on, he might very well be sacrificing himself to the man who killed his wife and son. If he didn't put them on, he might never get a chance to save the woman whom he was undoubtedly falling in love with.

Already fallen in love with, corrected a voice in his head, and he gave the voice a mental nod.

Yes, he'd already found that crazy, can't-live-without-her feeling.

And he knew what it was like to have no chance at all to save someone he loved.

It wasn't really much of a choice at all. He slid the cuffs to his wrists and snapped them shut.

"Show me they're secure," Dave ordered.

Graham lifted his hands and tugged them apart hard enough to bite punishingly into his skin.

"They're secure," he replied coolly.

"Good." Dave tucked his gun into his belt and stripped off his jacket. "I'm going to hang my coat over the cuffs, and we're going to take a walk."

"A walk?"

Dave shook his head. "No questions, unless they're about the weather or the Derby Reach Cardinals. You're going to stay on my right side—my gun side—just a little bit in front of me, but not so far in front that it looks forced. Got it?"

"Baseball, gun side, best buddies strolling through the neighborhood. Got it," Graham agreed.

And as Dave led him through the house and out the front door, Graham realized he didn't even have to ask where they were walking to.

Chapter Twenty-Four

Keira didn't even know she'd passed out until she was already struggling to pull herself into consciousness.

And wakefulness was unpleasant enough to make her wish she was still asleep.

Her eyes burned when she fought to open them. Wherever she was, it was dark, but that did nothing to relieve the sharp stab behind her lids. In fact, the rest of her hurt just as badly. Her head throbbed. And her throat ached and her wrists were on fire.

She was seated, but the chair dug into her shoulder blades and into the backs of her legs, too. She tried to adjust her body to ease some of the pain—*any* of it—and failed miserably. She was completely immobilized. And starting to sweat.

Where was she? What had Drew done? And *why*? Dear God… What about Calloway?

She might've cried, if she'd had the energy to do so.

"Water?"

The unfamiliar voice cut through the panic building up in her system. Abruptly, consuming something liquid was more important than being free, and she croaked out an assent.

"Please."

A cool metal rim reached her lips, tipped up, then drizzled a stream of water down her throat. Keira sucked it back thirstily, and it was pulled away far too soon.

"It's the sedative," the voice told her. "It'll make you crazy thirsty like that. But you don't want to drink too much, either, or it'll just come back up again."

"A little more?" Keira pleaded.

The unseen man sighed, but he did lift the water to her mouth again, very briefly.

"Good enough," he said. "In a few minutes, I'll turn on the lights, but the sedative will have given you a wicked headache, too, and the light will exacerbate it, I'm sure. In the meantime… are you as comfortable as can be, considering the circumstances?"

Keira wasn't sure how to answer. The speaker's question was genuine sounding. Almost kindly. It was the voice of someone's grandfather offering a child a sweet treat. But he clearly wasn't there to rescue her.

"Ms. Niles?"

"I've been better," she whispered hoarsely.

She could hear the shrug in his reply. "I suppose you probably have. Maybe we *all* have."

"Are you going to cut to the chase, or just keep stringing her along?" snapped another angrier voice.

Drew.

"We can do things my way, or you can leave," the first voice answered him in a restrained tone, then turned its attention back to Keira. "Should we try the dimmer?"

He didn't wait for her to answer. There was a click, and the room was bathed in a low, almost tolerable light. Keira squinted against the watering of her eyes. She was in a formal dining room, pushed into a corner away from a heavy wood table. And two figures stood in front of her.

The first was the new Drew—his expression set in a cruel scowl.

The other was an older man whom she didn't know, but who looked vaguely familiar. Even in the dim light, Keira could tell that he was a cut above average and he suited his voice perfectly. His gray hair was thick and styled, his suit well tailored and his skin ruddy in a just-returned-from-the-Bahamas kind of way. He offered her a smile.

"Okay?" he asked.

"Okay," Keira agreed, her voice still burning like fire.

"You know Mr. Bryant," he said pleasantly.

"But I don't think we've had the pleasure. I'm Councilman Henderson."

Councilman Henderson.

Keira's mind made the connection quickly. This was Calloway's father-in-law. The local politician with the wild-child daughter and the high ambitions and the reputation that needed protecting.

"You recognize my name, I see," he observed. "So that makes things a little bit easier. What I'm hoping is that we can make it *all* easy."

"Easy, how?" Keira wanted to know.

"Talking to her is a waste of time," Drew interrupted.

"If you weren't perpetually tired of wasting time," the older gentleman stated, "the painting would be in my hands and Holly would still be alive. I've told you before, there's doing things. And then there's doing things with finesse. Wouldn't you agree, Ms. Niles?"

"Finesse didn't bring you the girl," Drew retorted before Keira could answer. "I did."

"No," the other man argued, still sounding patient. "Whatever drugs you fed her brought her here. And I'm damned sure asking her nicely would have sufficed."

"You think *asking* her would have worked?"

"The girl is clearly in love with Graham and there's not much a girl won't do to protect the man she loves."

Keira opened her mouth to argue, but couldn't do it.

In love with him?

The realization made Keira's pulse race again, this time joyfully. Yes, she *did* love him, in that fast-and-hard, head-over-heels way that people wrote songs about. Everything about Calloway sang to her, made her thrum with life. The accident, the rescue...all of that had sped up the process, but there was no doubt in Keira's mind that the feelings were genuine. The very real likelihood of death intensified it all the more. And it made denying it impossible.

"I do love him," Keira said, hearing the truth of the statement in her voice. "And I'd lie to

protect him. But I don't know what you're talking about."

"You'd lie," Drew snarled. "But would you
die?"

Keira's reply was defiant. "Yes."

"Good."

He lunged at her, his hand drawn back for a
blow. Keira braced herself, but he didn't make
it close enough to hit her. Henry Henderson's
fist closed on the back of Drew's collar, and he
dragged the younger man back so forcefully that
he fell to the ground with a thud.

"You fail at *every* task I give you," Henderson
said, his voice betraying emotion for the first
time. "You have no patience, no fortitude, no
redeeming qualities. None. Now get out, guard
the door and give Ms. Niles and me a few minutes alone."

Remarkably, Drew didn't even argue. He just
pulled himself to his feet and slunk from the
room. Henderson waited until the French doors
were closed, then pulled out a chair from the
table, seated himself and crossed his legs. When

he turned his attention back to Keira, he was completely calm once more.

"Sometimes my sons forget who works for whom. My apologies," he said softly. "Now, where were we? Oh, right. Asking first certainly wouldn't have hurt. Ms. Niles, Graham Calloway has something I want. The man has been pouring his heart and soul out to you for days. He's either told you what I want to know, or he'll come here to rescue you and tell me himself. It's a win either way."

Keira barely heard what the man was saying. Her head was too busy trying to wrap around his first sentence.

His son.

No, not his son. His sons. *Plural.*

And Keira had a sinking feeling she knew who the other one was.

She needed to warn Calloway.

She stole a glance at Henry Henderson. He'd snapped up a newspaper from the table and turned his attention to what appeared to be a crossword puzzle.

Good.

Keira's hands twisted behind her back in search of a vulnerability in the rope. And after just a few seconds of trying, she found a loose spot, no bigger than her pinky finger. She just barely managed to keep from letting out a relieved cry.

She looked at Henderson again. He face was placid, as if he had no care outside of what word fit into fifty-one down.

I've got one for you, Keira thought. *What's an eleven-letter word for "drawing one's attention away from something"?*

D-I-S-T-R-A-C-T-I-O-N.

Keira closed her eyes for one second, dug her pinky into the loop, then opened her eyes again and asked, "What makes you so sure Calloway will come for me?"

Henderson blinked at her as if he'd completely forgotten her presence. Which she was damned well sure he hadn't.

"Pardon me, Ms. Niles?" he said.

She was also damned well sure he'd heard her the first time.

"There's a chance he won't come."

Henderson gave her a considering look. "Does he love you?"

Keira's face warmed. "I don't know."

Henderson shrugged. "I guess it doesn't matter. I believe he'll come, love or not. He'll feel responsible for you and obligation is a huge part of Graham's makeup. But if I'm wrong—which *is* a rare occurrence—I do have another ace or two up my sleeve."

The loop widened under Keira's attention.

"Like what?" she asked.

Henderson shook his head. "I think that's enough divulgence for the moment."

He went back to his crossword.

Dammit.

She had to keep him talking.

"What makes you think he even has this painting that you want?" she persisted. "He might not have it at all."

An amused smile tipped up the corner of the older man's mouth. "He has it."

Henderson took another sip of his drink and scratched something else onto the newspaper.

Keira had worked her finger in up to her knuckle already, and on the other side, she'd found another loose piece.

"How do you know?" she persisted.

Henderson folded the crossword in half, set it on the table and placed the cup on top.

"He had thirty-two million reasons to keep it," he told her.

It was Kiera's turn to blink slowly, and she had to force her fingers to keep working.

"Dollars?" she asked.

"That's right."

"But…"

"But what? You thought he was nothing more than an everyday hero, motivated by a general care for the well-being of mankind?" Henderson shook his head. "I'm afraid not."

Keira wiggled her wrists. There was definitely some extra room now.

"If Calloway had a thirty-two-million-dollar painting, and he cared so much about the money, why was he living in a shack?" she asked. "Why wouldn't he sell it?"

"He's greedy, not stupid. The first thing I did when my daughter died was to report it missing."

"The papers didn't say a word about it," Keira pointed out.

A few more inches, and at least one hand would be free.

Henderson smiled again. "They wouldn't."

"Why's that?"

"Because I didn't report it to the police."

Keira tugged a little harder on the rope and feigned confusion. "Why not the police? Wouldn't they be the best people to track it?"

"I'm afraid not." His tone was patronizing. "If a wanted criminal is going to sell a thirty-million-dollar painting, it's not going to be through the appropriate channels. The people I reported its theft to are the kind who monitor the darker side of things, Ms. Niles. People like your friend Drew."

"Drew?" she repeated.

One final little yank, and Keira felt the rope drop behind her. Quickly, she tucked her feet together under the chair to cover up the dangling evidence.

"The wannabe art thief," Henderson clarified.

"Well. That explains his wannabe expensive taste." Keira forced a laugh as she tried to take a casual look around.

The vase in the center of the table.

It was big and painted blue and probably worth more than a month's worth of rent. But it also looked breakable. Into small, sharp pieces, preferably.

She'd have to find out.

Chapter Twenty-Five

The house didn't just rest on top of its little hill. It loomed. Forbidding and hideous in its austerity.

It was the biggest one on the block—the one that all of the other houses in the neighborhood were modeled after. It wasn't that much older than its surrounding homes, but the lot was double the size. It was clearly designed not necessarily to stand out but to rule over.

Holly had told Graham that her mother had built the home, then given the rest of the property to her father to develop. A billion-dollar gift before the woman passed away and left everything else—the house, her fortune, her summer house overseas—to Holly herself.

Opulence.

It left a sour taste in Graham's mouth. It was one of the reasons the police believed he'd killed her. Killed *them.* Holly had spent the money— nearly every penny—and Graham, who had grown used to the *opulence*, was thrown into a rage.

The only thing left was the money in trust for Sam. The only way for Graham to get to that was to get rid of both of them.

Graham's jaw clenched involuntarily at the theory.

Money meant nothing to him. It never had, really. He'd gone into the medical field to help children who couldn't help themselves. He'd married Holly to help Sam.

But he'd wound up helpless, and the day he'd walked in and found Holly's body and Sam's blood…it was seared painfully into his memory.

The sirens had been close before Graham heard them.

Too close.

He'd known he ought to get up, slip out of the

house and pretend he hadn't been there at all. That he hadn't received the frantic phone call from Dave, hadn't come home from the motel and hadn't walked in on the devastating scene in the front hall of the home he'd shared with his wife and stepson.

Instead, he tore through the kitchen, bending down to open each low cupboard, calling out in a reassuring voice.

"Come out, come out, wherever you are!"

Where was the boy?

It was the only thing that stopped Graham from fleeing. He thought the boy had to be hiding somewhere, terrified. But where?

His heart had constricted as he moved past his wife's still form again, taking the stairs two at a time and forcing himself not to look back.

He might not have loved the woman the way he should, but in a million years, he would never have wished for something like that.

You tried to revive Holly, he'd reminded himself. *You really did. But you needed to find Sam.*

She'd been gone long before he got there.

Blood loss. Or the fall down the stairs. Even with his medical expertise, Graham couldn't say what had ultimately killed her.

Sam.

A crushing anger pushed at the corners of Graham's mind at what his stepson had witnessed.

He *had* to be a witness.

Graham couldn't even begin to accept the idea that the boy might've met the same fate as Holly. He loved the boy too much. Like nothing else in the world.

"Sammy!" he'd called as he'd opened the boy's bedroom door.

The usual assortment of Transformers and Lego and art supplies were strewn throughout the room. Graham saw none of them. The only thing that held his eye was the bed and the dark circle in the center of it.

No. Oh, no.

Graham knew blood when he saw it. It covered his hands and chest now, just as it covered his vision.

"Dr. Graham Calloway!" The cold, commanding voice had come from the doorway. "Hands where I can see them."

Numb, Graham lifted his arms and placed his palms on his head and turned around slowly.

"They're dead," he'd said to the officer in blue. "Holly and Sam are dead. You're too late."

The later-damning statement was out before he could stop it. It was also the last thing he'd said in that house the last time he'd been inside.

Until now.

"Am I going to have to drag you in there?" Dave's question forced Graham back to the present.

"No," he replied, his voice betraying more than a hint of the overwhelming, emotional drainage he'd experienced on that day four years earlier.

"Let's move, then."

"Are you going to uncuff me first?"

"I can't do that."

"Level with me," Graham said tiredly. "Are you taking me inside *just* to hand me straight over to Mike Ferguson, or are you taking me inside with any hope at all of saving the girl I love?"

The hesitation in the reply betrayed the truth even before the words did. "It has to be both."

"That's not even possible."

Dave shot a worried glance up toward the house. "I didn't have much of a choice here, Graham."

"There's always a choice."

Dave's face clouded with anger. "I know you think the past four years have been hard for you, and you only. But I lost something that day, too. Some *things*."

Graham rattled his cuffs emphatically. "What do you think *you* lost, Dave? *Your* freedom?"

"As a matter of fact, I did lose my freedom. Every person on the force knew about our friendship. I've never been promoted, never been given a second look for anything."

"You're blaming that on me?"

"My entire career was stalled when Holly died."

"Your entire career was stalled the second you started it, Dave," Graham snapped. "If I hadn't been there to bail you out of every bad thing you did, you'd be a two-bit criminal instead of a two-bit cop. Oh. Wait."

The other man narrowed his eyes. "I've made some bad choices, but I'm trying to make the right one now."

"By cuffing me?"

"If I don't cuff you, we don't get in. It's as simple as that."

"And what next? We get in there and you say you have to hand the keys to these cuffs to Ferguson because it's just that simple? Will you hand him the gun he uses to shoot me, too, and then blame *that* on simplicity?" The last question came out at a near yell, and Graham took a breath and tried to calm himself. "I thought you loved her, too."

"I did love her. Can we stop talking about this and go inside?"

Graham shook his head. "I don't think so. Not until you explain to me why you turned on me. Why you're helping the man who murdered Holly."

"He's not who you think he is."

"Now you're defending him? Dammit, Dave. You *loved* her. In a way that I couldn't. I never held that against you. I never even tried to stop it. So why do this?"

"It wasn't like that with Holly and me," Dave replied softly.

"You don't have to lie about it."

The other man exhaled loudly. "She was my sister."

It was the last thing Graham expected to hear. "Your what?"

"My sister."

"You don't have a damned sister."

"I don't anymore. But I did."

"Explain," Graham ordered.

"I don't think you really want to hear about it."

It was true. Part of him *didn't* want to hear. He didn't want to know what Dave was using to justify his actions. He didn't want to be asked to have any sympathetic feelings for anyone involved in Holly's and Sam's deaths. And he was sure that's where Dave was going with this.

He pushed past the desire to shut down.

"Explain," he repeated coldly.

Dave sighed again. "When my dad died, he left you cash for college. And even though you weren't his kid, I got it. You had a bond and I respected that. But he left me a different kind of legacy, Graham. He left a letter, confessing that he wasn't *my* real father at all, that my mother had an affair with a local politician. He didn't tell me his name. And I wasn't supposed to tell anyone that I knew. But it ate me up. Every waking moment, I thought about it. About who he might be. You remember how I was when my father died."

Graham *did* remember. He'd blamed the downward spiral on the senior Stark's death. It had made sense.

"How did you find out it was Henry?" he asked.

"Not long after you met Holly, you introduced us, and…I just knew it was him. Something in his eyes, his stance. It reminded me of myself. And he didn't even deny it when I confronted him."

"So you did what, blackmail him?"

"Not at first. I just threatened him with a lawsuit. He threatened me back. He said he knew people who would make me wish not only that I wasn't his biological son, but that I'd never been born at all. And I believed him. Completely."

"So Holly was a weaker target?"

"Not exactly."

Graham was growing impatient. "Stop being so taciturn, Dave. It's not helping either of us."

"Things got worse for me. The man I always thought of as my father was dead. The man who was my biological father threatened to kill *me*. So I did what I always did. I gambled away more money. I kept going until I owed my bookie tens of thousands. Until one of them—Mike Ferguson—sent someone after me."

Graham's anger reared its head again. "You knew him *before* he killed them? You—"

Dave cut him off. "I didn't *know* him, Graham. I never even saw him. I owed him money. And I told you that you didn't want to hear this."

Graham gritted his teeth. "Go on."

"The man he sent was named Drew Bryant,

and he didn't even ask me for the money I owed Ferguson. Instead, he told me he was my brother. Mine and Holly's. Another affair, another son," Dave said bitterly. "Henry took the term 'sow your wild oats' to an extreme, I guess. Drew convinced me that Henry owed us something. He'd been working for him and knew of a better way for us to get some money."

Drew Bryant.

He couldn't be Keira's boyfriend-potential Drew.

But he has to be.

"No coincidences," Graham muttered, then said a little more loudly, "After that, you went to Holly."

"After that, we went to Holly," Dave agreed. "She didn't even hesitate. She started paying us right away. Took the cash out of the bank that same day."

"And you were more than happy to take it."

"I owed money, Graham. A lot of it."

"So you thought it was okay to blackmail Holly?"

"We didn't *have* to blackmail her. She gave me the money willingly. She was thrilled to have brothers."

"You bankrupted her!"

"No. I paid my debt, thanked her, then didn't take a cent more. I told Drew I was out, and he agreed. So I kept my nose to the ground and washed my hands clean of Mike Ferguson. I paid my own way for a year," Dave explained. "But Drew kept taking money from her. I had no idea. Not until he came to me and told me she'd run out, and that he was planning on stealing the painting. I wanted to warn her. I was too late."

Bile rose in the back of Graham's throat. "Always about the money."

Dave looked as though he was about to say something else, but the door to the house where Graham once lived swung open, and a well-dressed, furious-looking man stepped onto the front veranda. He motioned angrily at Dave and Graham.

"Do I need to drag you in *now*?" Dave asked, displeasure clear in his inquiry.

Graham stared at the man on the stoop.

"Is that him?" he asked roughly.

If it was—if that was the man responsible for Holly's death—Graham wouldn't have to be dragged in. Just the opposite. It took all of his self-restraint to not run at the man, knock him down and wrap his throat with the chain on the cuffs and demand answers. Under the coat, he flexed his hands.

"That's Drew Bryant," Dave said. "Holly's brother, and mine."

"Where's Mike Ferguson?"

"Inside."

They moved forward together, and when they reached the porch, Drew Bryant gave Graham a dismissive once-over.

"This is the husband?" he asked, his tone as derisive as his expression.

"You know it is," Dave replied.

"I expected you to be more…impressive," the other man said.

Likewise, Graham thought, but he made himself stay quiet, assessing in silence.

He wasn't tall, but he wasn't short, either. His clothes were nice and his hair was tidy, but there was nothing remarkable about him at all. Graham couldn't see whatever it was that made Keira consider him boyfriend material, and he didn't know if that was a relief or not.

"Ready?" Dave prodded.

"Let's go," Graham replied grimly.

He started to step to the door, but Dave put a hand on his shoulder and muttered darkly, "He's not Mike Ferguson. But I bet you're going to wish he was."

Chapter Twenty-Six

Keira waited until Henderson had immersed himself back in the crossword puzzle before she heaved herself to her feet and dove for the vase. Henderson reacted quickly, leaping up from his chair and pushing Keira away from her intended target. But her hand still managed to bump it, and she sent it rolling.

As the vase lumbered along, flashing blue on brown, Keira used the momentum given to her by Henderson's shove to propel herself under the table. When the older man bent down to grab her, she kicked out one bare foot, smacking him solidly in the forehead. He fell to his knees, but came at her again immediately. She struck him once more, this time in the chin. When he lunged a third time, Keira grabbed ahold of two chair legs and forced them together with as much strength as she could muster. They put a temporary barrier between her and the man hell-bent on getting to her. When he tried to shove the chairs out of his way, Keira gave one of them a push. It clipped Henderson in the eye, and he finally fell back, his hand on his brow.

"Drew!" he hollered.

And Keira thumped the chair forward again, harder than before. This time, the blow was hard enough to send him flying. He righted himself and shot her a furious glare.

"You little—"

Whatever he'd been about to say was lost in the sound of the vase hitting the hardwood floor and shattering.

Keira covered her eyes as the shards flew around her. She counted to three in her head, hoping that would give the porcelain enough time to settle, then opened her eyes in search of a big enough piece of vase to use as a weapon.

But Henderson was a step ahead of her. He already had a pointed chunk of porcelain gripped in one hand and was crawling toward Keira.

For a second, she was frozen to the spot, mesmerized by the gruesome sight in front of her.

Little pieces of blue flecked Henderson's face and around each of them was a dot of crimson. A bigger slice had jabbed into his shoulder, and from that, a steady stream of blood oozed.

He paused on the other side of the chairs.

Move!

It only took Keira a heartbeat to obey the command in her head. She scurried back, hit the wall behind her, then moved left, bringing herself closer to the door.

Bits of blue porcelain scraped underneath her as she slid along the floor, and she ignored the way they dug at her.

Three more feet.

But Henderson was nearly on his feet again and almost as close to her as she was to the exit.

Keira snapped up a piece of broken vase and

held it out in front of her as she grabbed the door frame and pulled herself up.

"You might as well drop it. I'm bigger than you and stronger than you. I'm not afraid of hurting you. And I will," Henderson said, and Keira marveled that he somehow still managed to sound calm in spite of his threatening words. "I'm going to overpower you in seconds."

"And you're going to lose an eye in the process," Keira retorted.

"We'll see."

As he jumped toward her, the French doors flew open, and Henderson took advantage of Keira's momentary surprise. One of his arms closed around her, pinning her arms to her sides, and the other came up to press his own shard of sharp porcelain directly into her jugular.

GRAHAM STARED IN horror at the scene in front of him, the truth unfolding in his mind.

The gray-haired man—covered in abrasions and looking like a poorly aged thug—was absolutely someone he knew. Well. And he had

Keira in a death grip and showed no signs of letting her go.

He's inches away from cutting her throat.

"Henry…"

"Mike," the man corrected. "Ferguson. At least as far as this little scenario is concerned."

Graham's stomach caved in; his head boomed with the revelation.

His father-in-law was a well-respected member of the community. A city councilman, with power and influence, and a reputation sullied only by Holly's exploits.

And a murderer.

Graham's mouth hung open, a dozen unable-to-be-articulated questions on the tip of his tongue.

Then he realized the answers didn't matter. Not right that second anyway.

Graham recovered from his momentary inability to move and strode forward, forgetting his cuffs, forgetting the two men on either side of him, forgetting everything except Keira and her safety.

"Stop!" his father-in-law commanded.

A little bead of blood formed under the point he had pressed to Keira's neck, and Graham paused. There was a responding shuffle from behind him, and he quickly found himself grasped by Drew on one side and Dave on the other. He made no attempt to throw them off. All of his attention was on the girl and the man who held her.

"Let her go," Graham said, not bothering to acknowledge his captured state.

"Unlikely," Henry replied.

His voice was full of the scorn that had characterized him so well over the two years Graham had been married to the man's daughter. Graham paused, taking stock of the situation. He knew Keira was being used, not just as bait now, but also as leverage. He knew also that he was faster than the older man and he was sure he could incapacitate the two men who held him.

But can you do both things quickly enough and effectively enough to win?

Maybe, maybe not.

Henry probably wouldn't kill her, given a

choice. It would take away that bit of leverage he had. But if he felt as though he didn't *have* a choice...

There was a click behind him and Graham knew he'd wasted too much time thinking about it. One of the two men holding him had cocked a gun.

"It's aimed at *her* head, not yours," Henry said. "Confirm that for me, Ms. Niles."

Keira's eyes lifted to a spot behind Graham, then she met his eyes and inclined her head. Just that slight nod was enough to draw more blood from her throat.

"Stop." Graham was pleading and he didn't care. "Don't hurt her."

Henry smiled. "Are you going to offer to take her place?"

"Yes," Graham replied right away.

Henry's smile widened. "I'd like to say I expected something less cliché from you, but it would be a lie. It's just the kind of bleeding heart offer I *would* expect from you."

"Because I care about something other than money and the public eye?"

"Because caring is your weakness. And that weakness is what got you in trouble in the first place. It's what made you marry my daughter when you should have stayed away and what got you accused of murder. It's what's going to make you give me what *I* want now."

Graham balked at the derogatory simplification of his personality. "I'm not giving you anything."

"Then I'll kill her," Henry replied with a shrug.

Graham forced himself to sound unmoved by the statement. "Like you killed Holly and Sam?"

His father-in-law sighed. "That was an unfortunate accident."

Graham's jaw clenched at the man's casual dismissal of the loss of life, as did his stomach. Before he could speak again, the man with the gun interjected.

"I'll shoot her," he offered. "Maybe in the hand, just to show you how serious we are."

"If you hurt her, I'll have no reason at all to help you," Graham snapped.

His father-in-law sighed. "Drew. I don't want you to shoot anyone at the moment. And, Graham, you should know by now that I never place all my bets on one number."

"You took every other thing from me," Graham countered.

Henry opened his mouth, but suddenly, Keira was alive in the older man's arms. She threw an elbow into his stomach and stomped down on his foot. Henry released her with a grunt and dropped the shard of porcelain to the ground. He reached for her, but Keira was too fast. She darted across the room and reached Graham just as Drew fired off a wild shot.

"I told you *not* to shoot in here," Henry snarled.

"You said not to shoot *anyone*," Drew corrected.

The older man strode toward the younger one, and Graham decided now was the only opportunity they might have to run. The one thing between him and the door was Dave. He met the police officer's eyes.

"Hit me," Dave instructed, just loud enough to be heard.

Graham didn't have to be told twice. He pulled his still-bound hands together and rammed them into Dave's gut. As the smaller man fell to the floor, he dropped the keys to the cuffs and Graham snagged them.

Graham grabbed Keira's hand and dragged her through the French doors and out into the hall. He was glad to see nothing had been done to change the decor in the home. Everything was exactly as he remembered it. Including a large, heavy table positioned against the wall just outside the dining room. Swiftly, he got behind it and pushed—with considerable effort—so that it blocked the doors. Then he clasped Keira's hand once more and set off at a run without looking back.

Chapter Twenty-Seven

Keira raced to keep up with Calloway as he tore through the large home with easy familiarity. They hit the front door in moments, but once they were there, Calloway paused, glanced through the curtains and shook his head.

"Henry's got a man out there in his car," he told her. "I can see him from here."

"Out the back, then?" Keira breathed, her throat still raw.

"Probably just as risky."

Behind them, she could hear the thump of the three men as they fought through the small blockade.

"I've got an idea," Calloway said.

He yanked on her hand, and they moved from the entryway, through the family room, then paused at the bottom of the stairs.

"C'mon!" Calloway called loudly. "The master bedroom!" Then he put his hand on her shoulder and leaned in to whisper, "Wait here."

He thundered up the stairs, two at a time, his feet hitting the steps, loud and hard. When he reached the top, he turned around and tiptoed back down. Without asking permission, Calloway slid his arms around Keira and lifted her from the ground. In complete silence, he carried her into the kitchen.

Moments later, the bang of booted feet and deep voices carried through the house.

They're free.

But Calloway ignored them as he set Keira on the countertop.

"Just a sec," he murmured.

Keira watched in amazement as he crouched low, found a loose floorboard, lifted it, then reached into it. With a heave, he pulled on something inside and an old-fashioned trapdoor squeaked open. Calloway held it up.

"In," he commanded. "There's a railing on your right."

Keira didn't bother to argue. She stepped down into the darkness, her hand finding the railing immediately. She used it to guide her all the way to the bottom of the stairs. As she reached the floor, the light above her cut out, and the door clicked shut. In seconds, she felt Calloway reach her side. They stood there wordlessly, shoulder to shoulder, for a long minute.

"Wine cellar?" Keira finally whispered, just to break the silence.

"Man cave," Calloway corrected, just as softly.

He moved away briefly, then there was a click, and a blue-and-yellow neon sign came to life in one corner.

Vaguely, Keira was aware that her surroundings were similar to those of Calloway's hidden cabin. Wood panel walls and rustic decor.

Mostly, though, all she was aware of was Calloway.

It had only been two hours—maybe three— since she'd seen him. It seemed like a lifetime. She had to feel him. Touch him. Breathe him in and hold him there.

She slipped her hands around his shoulders, molded her body to his and tipped her face up expectantly. Calloway didn't disappoint her. He pressed his palms into the small of her back, pulling her impossibly closer, and tilted down to push his lips into hers.

Calloway's mouth was perfect. *He* was perfect. Perfectly imperfect. Perfectly *hers.*

For the duration of the kiss, the world disappeared. No crazy past haunting them, no violent men hunting them.

The men. The brothers, she remembered, and pulled away reluctantly.

"Dave Stark and Drew—the man I thought I was running to—they're *his* sons," Keira said in a rush. "And Holly's brothers."

He cupped her cheek. "I know. Dave explained it."

"So you were right," Keira added, "About there being no coincidences."

"Sometimes I wish I was wrong," Calloway replied grimly.

He kissed her once more, then moved across the room toward a raised, blank space on the far wall.

"That's just panel drywall," he said. "I sealed up a window, and it's still there on the other side. It comes out in the side yard."

"You want to break through?" Keira asked. "You don't think they'll hear it upstairs?"

"It's probably our only chance."

Calloway had already snagged a hammer from the tool chest. He angled the claw under the drywall and pulled at the points where the nails had been hammered in. It was a nearly silent endeavor, and in just a few minutes, he'd freed a quarter of the drywall. When he paused to tap the edges, several pieces of the chalky material crumbled away.

"Not too bad," he stated, sounding pleased.

The second half was even easier. The loose

bits on the side Calloway had already pried off seemed to have compromised the structural integrity of the one he was taking apart now. It only took a few moments for the whole thing to come down.

The windowpane was covered in grime, and the latch squealed in protest as Calloway forced it back.

Keira sent up a hurried prayer that it would open in spite of its worse-for-wear appearance, then watched anxiously as Calloway put both hands on the glass and pushed. It resisted for only a second before it flew to the side, sending in a waft of fresh air.

Keira inhaled deeply.

"I'll go first," Calloway told her. "Then I'll help you through."

He grabbed the edge of the dirty sill, his biceps flexing as he pulled himself up. He went out quickly, then jabbed his hands back through.

Keira let his warm hands close on her wrists and drag her up. For a relieved moment, they stood toe-to-toe in the window well. It was short-lived.

Henderson's deep, calm voice carried through the air. "And here I was, thinking you might actually get away."

Keira looked up. All three men stood staring down at them. Drew's eyes were full of muted fury. Dave's were almost apologetic. And Henry's...they were bright with anticipation.

"This is it, isn't it?" he asked, sounding nearly gleeful.

Calloway didn't answer, and Keira though that was a bad sign for them. And Henderson seemed to take it as encouragement, too.

"Should we go back into the house?" His question was far too pleasant.

Calloway clearly thought so, too. "Are you giving us a choice?"

"Not even a little bit," Henderson told them. "Back the way you came."

They all slipped through the window—first Drew, then Keira and Graham, then Dave and finally Henry Henderson.

ONCE THEY WERE in the basement, Graham stood protectively in front of Keira. His father-in-law took a slow look around the dim room.

"Amazing," said Henry. "My wife *built* this house and I had no idea this room was down here."

"Maybe there was a good reason for that," Graham retorted.

Henderson shot him one of his usual impassive stares. "Yes. I'm sure there was. She probably planned on using it as a place to hide her wine. She was rather fond of it. Just like Holly."

"You have no right to say her name," Graham growled. "You lost that right when you took her life."

Henry sighed. "It was never my intention to harm her physically. It wouldn't have happened if Drew had taken care of incapacitating her properly in the first place."

Drew spoke up. "How was I supposed to know she had such a high tolerance for prescription drugs?"

"So you're blaming the murder on him?"

Henry shrugged. "Partially. I pulled the trigger because she got in the way. All I wanted was the painting. It was rightfully mine. But my wife somehow deemed Holly a better choice."

How the other man could be so blasé about the murders of his own daughter and his own grandson—murders the man had just admitted to committing himself—was completely beyond Graham.

"Speaking of the painting…" Drew piped up again.

Without bothering to think about the consequences, Graham turned and swung a fist. He hit Drew straight in the face and the other man collapsed to the floor, his eyes rolled back in his head and blood dripped from his nose.

His father-in-law took a quick step toward the unconscious body, but Graham was faster. His hand shot out and caught Henry straight in the throat. He backed the older man to the far wall.

"Are you going to *do* something, Stark?" Henry asked.

The policeman shook his head. "I'd rather not."

Graham smiled coldly. "Do you know what that is behind me?"

He watched as the man's brown eyes—so like Holly's, so like Sam's—traveled up and went wide as they found the framed piece of art, sandwiched between a Budweiser ad and a Rolling Stones poster.

"That's it," Graham said. "The thirty-plus million-dollar painting you killed them for, you sick son of—"

"Just her," Henderson corrected.

Graham went still. "What the hell does that mean?"

"I didn't kill Sam," Henry stated casually.

"That's a lie," Graham replied in a hoarse whisper. "I saw the blood."

"There was blood," Henry agreed. "Lots of blood."

"Sam is dead."

"He's not. If you let me get my phone from my pocket, I'd be happy to show you."

Graham wanted to tell the other man where he could shove his phone, but a small part of him filled with hope. He tried to fight the burgeoning emotion. He failed.

"Show me."

He loosened his grip just enough that the other man could reach into his coat. He pulled out a smartphone, held it up and punched in a pass code. In moments, a picture flooded the small screen.

A little boy with perfect blond curls and oh-so-familiar brown eyes. He was bigger, and not really smiling in the carefree way Graham had always remembered him. But…

"That's impossible," Graham breathed.

He couldn't take his eyes from the photograph.

"You know it's him," Henry said.

It was. Graham was sure.

"How?" he asked.

"The kid took a through and through," the older man explained. "Holly's second bullet. Went through her abdomen and nicked Sam in a pretty big artery. And you were right about the blood. Way more than I thought one small person could lose. Drew and I bandaged him up pretty tight, took him to a retired doctor I knew. Saved the kid's life."

"Why would you hold that back all these years?" Graham asked.

"What good would it do to tell anyone he was alive?" Henry countered. "Besides which, it made the police search for you that much harder. And I thought the guilt—or the desire for revenge—might get to you eventually. Bring you home."

"Where is he?"

"Close."

"Take me to him," Graham said.

"Let me have the painting, and I will."

"Sam first. We can come back for the painting."

Henry sighed. "Fine."

"Get Drew's gun, Keira," Graham ordered.

She'd been silent, letting the scene unfold, and now she shot an uncertain glance toward Dave.

"He's not going to stop you," Graham assured her.

Dave nodded, and Keira moved. But Graham had misjudged the other man's alertness, and as Keira's hand almost closed on the weapon, Drew sat straight up, twisted and pulled the girl forcefully into his lap.

"Put him down, Calloway. Or I'll shoot the girl," Drew announced coldly.

"He'll shoot me anyway," Keira stated.

Graham's heart squeezed. He couldn't lose her. He couldn't lose Sam again.

"I have to take the chance that he won't," he said. "I love you too much."

"I love you, too," she whispered back.

Drew snarled, "Enough!"

Graham's arms fell to his sides, and Henry shoved past him, his hands already reaching for the painting. But as he moved, Graham's foot shot out. The older man stumbled, straight into Keira and Drew. The gun flew from Drew's grasp. It discharged loudly, and a *riiiiiip* echoed through the basement.

"No," Henry gasped.

Graham's eyes followed his gaze, straight up to the painting. To the brand-new bullet-sized hole that adorned its center.

And Graham smiled.

Epilogue

Five Weeks Later

"Do you think the smoke has finally cleared?" Keira asked, unsure if she was hoping for a yes or for a no.

Graham seemed to sense the flip-flop nature of her question.

"Maybe," he replied. "Maybe not. We can wait here awhile longer. Your work said to take the time you need, and I'm not in a hurry, either."

He uncurled himself from the brand-new, built-for-two rocking chair on the front porch of the old log cabin. He stretched, wide shoulders flexing in a way that made Keira's blood heat up in spite of the chilly air.

"Is he asleep yet?" she wondered out loud.

Graham smiled, that same silly, dopey, love-filled grin that he always grinned whenever Sam was concerned.

"I was just going to check," he told her.

Keira watched his back as he retreated into the cabin, admiring the view.

My Mountain Man, she thought affectionately.

He was almost always at ease now that his father-in-law was behind bars. His own name had been officially cleared, too. Dave was let off with a slap on the wrist. And Sam… He'd spent four years shuffled between nannies, with—thankfully—little direct contact with his grandfather and the man's underhanded activities. He was as serious a kid as Keira had ever met, but he smiled a little more every day. And twice this week, Keira had heard him drop the word *Daddy* when referring to Calloway.

No, she decided. *I'm not in a huge hurry to get out of here.*

GRAHAM PEELED BACK the curtain to the closet-turned-tiny-bedroom and gazed down lovingly at his kid. His living, breathing kid. He'd never get tired of staring at that perfect little face. He was so glad that Sam had been spared the darker parts of Graham's father-in-law's life.

Graham's heart swelled, gratitude and awe nearly overwhelming him as it did almost every time he took stock of his life.

Accused murderer. Redeemed father. Loving husband.

Well, soon-to-be husband, if the ring in his pocket worked like he thought it would.

"Calloway?"

Keira's soft voice made him turn.

She'd stepped into the cabin, dropped her jacket and stood in front of the blissfully small bed they shared every night in nothing but one of his T-shirts. His favorite outfit.

"Sam's okay?" she asked.

"Perfect," he replied.

Keira smiled. "Like always."

"Like you," Graham teased, happy when she blushed.

He walked to her, wrapped her in his arms and kissed her thoroughly, just to make the pink in her cheeks brighten even more.

"Hey," he murmured when he pulled away. "Can I ask you something?"

"Anything."

He dug his hand into his pocket, yanked out the little box and balanced it on his palm. "On a sliding scale…how happy are you that you drove into a snowstorm, got rescued by a mountain man and almost got killed by a corrupt politician?"

Keira's eyes lit up. "Ten out of ten!"

Graham grinned and kissed her again, secure that fate was well in hand.

* * * * *

MILLS & BOON®

Why shop at millsandboon.co.uk?

Each year, thousands of romance readers find their perfect read at millsandboon.co.uk. That's because we're passionate about bringing you the very best romantic fiction. Here are some of the advantages of shopping at www.millsandboon.co.uk:

* **Get new books first**—you'll be able to buy your favourite books one month before they hit the shops

* **Get exclusive discounts**—you'll also be able to buy our specially created monthly collections, with up to 50% off the RRP

* **Find your favourite authors**—latest news, interviews and new releases for all your favourite authors and series on our website, plus ideas for what to try next

* **Join in**—once you've bought your favourite books, don't forget to register with us to rate, review and join in the discussions

Visit **www.millsandboon.co.uk**
for all this and more today!